The Hamburg Score

Viktor Shklovsky

THE HAMBURG SCORE

Translated from the Russian by Shushan Avagyan

DALKEY ARCHIVE PRESS

Originally published in Russian by Izdatelstvo Pisatelei v Leningrade as *Gamburgsky Schyot* in 1928.

Names: Shklovsky, Viktor, 1893-1984, author. | Avagyan, Shushan, translator.
Title: The Hamburg score / by Viktor Shklovsky.
Other titles: Gamburgsky schyot. English
Description: First Dalkey Archive edition. | Victoria, TX : Dalkey Archive Press, 2017. | Originally published in Russian by Izdatelstvo Pisatelei v Leningrade in 1928.
Identifiers: LCCN 2016047018 | ISBN 9781628971675 (pbk. : alk. paper)
Subjects: LCSH: Russian literature--20th century--History and criticism.
Classification: LCC PG2950 .S5613 2017 | DDC 891.709/004--dc23
LC record available at https://lccn.loc.gov/2016047018

Partially funded by a grant by the Illinois Arts Council, a state agency. This publication was effected under the auspices of the Mikhail Prokhorov Foundation TRANSCRIPT Programme to Support Translations of Russian Literature.

www.dalkeyarchive.com
Victoria, TX / McLean, IL / Dublin

Dalkey Archive Press publications are, in part, made possible through the support of the University of Houston-Victoria and its programs in creative writing, publishing, and translation.

Printed on permanent/durable acid-free paper

CONTENTS

TRANSLATOR'S NOTE

The titles of Viktor Shklovsky's books, even the chapter headings and subheadings, always stand out, manifesting a readiness to take surprisingly bold risks. They are objects in themselves and have a life of their own. "The object calls for the making of the contemporary in contemporaneity," wrote El Lissitzky and Ilya Erenburg in the first issue of *Veshch*. "Amid a stifling atmosphere, drained Russia, fattened and slumbering Europe, there is only one call: STOP DECLARING AND REFUTING, MAKE THINGS!"[1] This was the call of the decade: to construct new kinds of objects and to forge new ways of organizing socially—to build a new society in post-revolutionary Russia. Shklovsky was both a participant in the Russian avant-garde literary movement and a theorist of the new literary form. Extremely knowledgeable in the literary traditions and schools of the past, he vehemently reacted to the imitation and copying of old forms, which he critically called "inertial forms." Traditionalism and "quoted themes" corrupted the new literature, Shklovsky argued, addressing the new generation of writers in *The Hamburg Score*: "There is no need to go after old literature like a cyclist riding after a tramcar. You have the electricity!"

---

1   *Veshch/Gegenstand/Objet* (Object: International Review of Contemporary Art) was a trilingual journal edited by El Lissitzky and Ilya Erenburg, published in two issues by Skythen Verlag, Berlin, in 1922.

The Hamburg Score belongs to Shklovsky's most prolific and experimental period at the end of the height of OPOYAZ, the Society for the Study of Poetic Language, which he helped found in 1914. He was moving away from long, semi-academic articles and searching for alternative and hybrid forms of writing such as *the critical feuilleton* (on how to write a feuilleton and how to write about a feuilleton) or *the novel-essay* (which fused two distinct forms, the novel and the essay) to revolutionize both the act of writing and the perception of the act of writing. The main "characters" in *The Hamburg Score* are the new form—the feuilleton, Viktor Shklovsky, and *The Hamburg Score* (see "A Review of This Book"). In this regard, Shklovsky is not merely a writer's writer, as he claimed in the book, but also a critic's critic and a theorist's theorist. And his "object-oriented" or "material-oriented" text offers a radically different sociopolitical conception of objects, our relation to them, and their relation to us.

"The Hamburg score is a very important concept," wrote Shklovsky in the preface of the book and proceeded to illustrate Aesopically why the strange concept was so important. Still, when he delivered the manuscript of the book to the Writers' Publishing House in Leningrad in 1928, he probably had no idea that the title would become such an influential term and completely materialize in the Russian language as it did. "Судить по гамбургскому счету," meaning to judge with absolute fairness, to make a judgment without concession or compromise, became a critical expression in Russian literary and film circles in the 1950s, and soon after spread into other realms. Ironically, this was due to the fact that Shklovsky had been dangerously criticized by Stalinist ideologues during the campaign against the "Cosmopolites" after World War II, when the writer and editor-in-chief of the journal *Novy Mir* Konstantin Simonov condemned *The Hamburg Score* for being the theoretical base of an "antipatriotic system of appraisal" that was "hostile to Soviet art."[2] The title of the book and the term itself seemed especially provocative during the postwar era (though nearly twenty years had passed after the book's publication) as it ran counter to Soviet popular anti-German sentiments, among other things. (It should be pointed out that the choice of Hamburg for the eponymous phrase was rather arbitrary; it was based on an anecdote that Shklovsky had heard at the writers' restaurant in Herzen House.) In his attempt to discredit Shklovsky, Simonov quoted the preface of *The Hamburg Score* line by line, accusing the critic of his influence on other "reactionary" and "bourgeois" critics who "tried to undermine real Soviet literature." It is a miracle that Shklovsky survived this kind of criticism, but later he humorously recalled: "A year after Simonov's article appeared in print, I read the following sentence in a conversation of collective farmworkers in one of [Valentin] Ovechkin's sketches: 'We'll fix a Hamburg score for him now!' As far as I can remember, the conversation was about a neighbor who had been showing off. They'd remembered the term and its meaning."[3] By then, the condemned phrase had already entered the common language of the day as a popular buzzword in social and political discourse.

And yet, the concept, as conceived by Shklovsky, belonged to the sphere of art, and more specifically literature: "In sport ... the Olympic score is the real score because there are indices against which one can check. In art, however, the rules of scoring are often violated, and the person who was declared a champion suddenly ends up on a stand for discounted books. So this means that we need some kind of a score without pretensions."[4]

2   In the March 1949 issue of *Novy Mir*.
3   Qtd. in Viktor Konetsky, "We Could Do Without Names—V. B. Shklovsky," in *Ekho* (St. Petersburg, 1998).
4   *Ibid.*

Applying this method of determining true worth to the Russian literature of his time, which he did with reasonableness and authenticity, Shklovsky arrived at the only possible conclusion: the most brilliant avant-garde writer among the great Russian writers of the twentieth century had to be Velimir Khlebnikov (1885–1922).[5] It was Khlebnikov, the creative genius behind the Russian Futurist movement, whose transrational language (*zaum*) came closest to transmitting life as it had never been experienced before, something that everyday speech could never aspire to. Khlebnikov was an exceptional poet, and time has proven that he was indeed "the king of time," as he was once proclaimed by his Futurist friends. "As to we who 'love to be astonished'"[6]—we are *still* astonished with Khlebnikov's sound and nearly impossible-to-read verses, that snatch the rules of grammar and syntax from under our feet and "exorcise through laughter" (Khlebnikov) our bewilderment at the new words.

5   Shklovsky's first pamphlet *The Resurrection of the Word* (1914) was about transrational language (*zaum*), and Khlebnikov was the first in the line up of Futurist poets: "They either create a new word from an old root (Velimir Khlebnikov, Elena Guro, Vasili Kamensky, Vasilisk Gnedov), or crack it with rhyme, like Mayakovsky, or use a rhythm with a wrong stress pattern (Aleksei Kruchyonykh). New, living words are created."
6   Lyn Hejinian, *My Life* (Sun & Moon Press, 1987).

ACKNOWLEDGMENTS

For enabling me to see this work through, I am infinitely grateful to Rebecca Chase and Paula Ressler for their unconditional welcome and for turning their home into the most hospitable space for translational adventures. This project would not have come to fruition without their warmth, generosity, and friendship. I also wish to thank Rebecca Saunders for the long walks along the lake in Chicago and conversations that sustained me with intellectual dialogue and new insights. I have benefited greatly from the Milner Library at Illinois State University, and I am particularly thankful to the literature and languages librarian Jean MacDonald for providing me with access to the collections of the library and a workspace. I would not have been able to complete this extraordinary project without the support of the American University of Armenia and the Calouste Gulbenkian Foundation. Finally, I owe my greatest thanks to my partner, Arpi Adamyan, for being a continuing source of inspiration and strength, and to my parents for their encouragement.

S. Avagyan
July 23, 2016

THE HAMBURG SCORE

PREFACE

The Hamburg score is a very important concept.

All wrestlers cheat in matches and fall on their shoulder blades at the behest of the entrepreneurs.

But once a year wrestlers gather at a pub in Hamburg.

They wrestle behind closed doors and curtained windows.

It is a long, hard, and ugly fight. But this is the only way to determine their true worth—to prevent them from getting corrupted.

We need a Hamburg score in literature.

According to the Hamburg score, Serafimovich and Veresaev don't exist.

They don't reach the city.

In Hamburg, Bulgakov is down on the mat.

Babel is a lightweight.

Gorky is questionable (often out of form).

Khlebnikov was the champion.

NOTEBOOK

WHAT WAS REAL LITERATURE ACCORDING TO PUSHKIN

SOVREMENNIK (THE CONTEMPORARY)

IT WAS A JOURNAL published by Pushkin and berated by Bulgarin in *Severnaya pchela* (*Northern Bee*). Let me quote some article headings and characteristic phrases:

"The friends of the editors are excessively praised in the other contemporary journals" (Issue #213).

"Neither Schiller nor Goethe participated in the petty fights of the scribblers, and they didn't belong to any party." "They can keep reassuring themselves—Pushkin's period has ended." "The decline of Pushkin's talent ..." (Issue #216). "I am annoyed with Pushkin" (Issue #146). In general, Bulgarin was not hounding Pushkin. He was only giving him some guiding advice.

Sovremennik almost never published plotted prose. In its first year it published Gogol's "The Carriage" and "The Nose." The latter was published with a note from the editor.[7]

On the other hand, the journal published "A Journey to Arzrum," "The Works of Georgi Konisky" (including long quotations from the Archbishop's writings).

A range of articles; letters from Paris; the notes of Nadezhda Durova; an article on the probability theory; an article on the

---

7 The editor's note praised the short story: "N. V. Gogol did not wish to publish this piece for a long time, but we found so many surprising, fantastic, humorous, and original things in it that we persuaded him to let us share the pleasure that his manuscript gave us with the public.—Ed."

partisan war; historical anecdotes; a translation of the adventures of a boy who was taken prisoner by Native Americans; a journey through Moscow.

There were, of course, no novels in *Sovremennik*. But there was an article titled "How We Write Novels" (signed by F. S.).

This phenomenon cannot be explained by the fact that there was no Russian prose at this time, or that the public was not interested in prose. Quite the opposite. We find out from Gogol's article in that same issue of *Sovremennik* that, "People are mostly reading novels, frigid, boring stories, and it has become quite clear that people are generally indifferent to poetry."[8]

And yet half of the journal was poetry.

Sovremennik was an inventive journal. It searched for a transition to a new kind of prose that focused on the material.

We can't even say that the documentary prose published in *Sovremennik* was thematically different from the plotted prose of that period. Rather, the documentary extracts coincided thematically with the plotted prose and cautioned it.

For example, the quotations from Georgi Konisky describing the executions of the Cossacks textually coincide with Gogol's *Taras Bulba*.

There was a fight between "the details" and generalization, between fiction and fact. It was rather intense:

> Simply write your own notes without chasing after fantasy and without calling them a novel. Then your book will have the same appeal as any chronicle and, what is more, people will read it not with the intention of reading a novel, as that kind of a mindset is disastrous for anything that you consider

8   "O dvizhenii zhurnalnoi literatury" [The Movement of Journalistic Literature], *Sovremennik*, Issue #1.

to be the best in your work! Don't be fooled by success either: readers look for hints at their own names in your novels when they aren't looking for a novel … (*Sovremennik*, Issue #3)

THE PRINT RUN OF OUR JOURNALS

The print run of *Literaturnaya gazeta* (*The Literary Gazette*), according to Barsukov, was "hardly a hundred copies." Pushkin wrote in this journal.

The print run of *Teleskop* (*Telescope*), where Belinsky wrote, was so low that the publisher consciously sabotaged the journal by publishing Chaadaev's "Philosophical Letter" in the fifteenth issue.

The journal *Yevropeets* (*The European*) with names such as Zhukovsky, Yazykov, Baratynsky, and Pushkin had about fifty subscribers.

Sovremennik reached up to five hundred subscribers. *Biblioteka dlya chtenia* (*Library for Reading*) was also successful, for which it should certainly not be reproached.

Mirgorod and *Arabeski* (*Arabesques*) had no subscribers.

ABOUT BULGARIN

We know him from his fight against Pushkin and against aristocracy in the name of the mass reader.

Bulgarin's report to General Potapov is a clever piece. It perfectly describes the middle- and lower-class reader.

Bulgarin himself was not a plebeian. According to a certificate issued on May 9, 1826 by the Military Governor of St. Petersburg

Mikhail Kutuzov, "Second Lieutenant Faddei Bulgarin is a nobleman from the Minsk province; his father owned seven hundred
and fifty souls of male serfs …"

In 1832 Baron Rosen wrote to Shevyryov: "Did Pushkin tell
you that Bulgarin is trying to obtain the title of Prince? He is
claiming that he is Prince Scanderbeg Buggarn."

But, of course, Bulgarin's origins and his pretensions do not
determine the class that he served.

Pushkin's aristocracy is conventional and literary.

The real aristocrat, Vyazemsky, has little respect for his lineage.
Ibrahim Petrovich Hannibal was a Negro—a sore point for the
aristocracy, which is hardly remedied with exoticism. Pushkin's
aristocracy is linked with Byron's biography and appears to be a
part of his literary image. Pushkin's heraldic lion is very young.
It was Paul I who put Russian heraldry in order.

The Russian boyars didn't have any coats of arms before that.

They used randomly engraved stones as their seals. The seals
weren't always clear and legible. For instance, a bird with a phal-
lus transformed into a bird on a cannon and became the coat of
arms of the Smolensk province.

A FEW WORDS ABOUT
VYACHE POLONSKY

There are witty sayings that are formed on their own: "not a critic, but a cryptic," "not *LEF*, but bluff." They are so banal that it is not even worth using them.

It is vulgar.

It is also not appropriate to fill up four of the eight columns of a feuilleton with quotations.

Especially if you want to prove that the quotation is an example of bad writing and that one shouldn't publish such things.

It is not appropriate to start a critical article with: "I opened the book," "I was interested in," "I leafed through," or "I glanced through."

You can't start a review of a play by saying: "I walked into the theater and sat down on an armchair."

All of this is extremely weak, because you cannot start reading a book without opening it.

Therefore, you cannot consider, for example, the works published by V. Polonsky as the notes of a journalist.

The articles are incompetent and unprofessional to say the least.

They are the writings of an administrator, and not a journalist.

And a writing administrator often resembles a theater fireman who sings.

One ought to get rid of the old general's habit of calling people "unknown."

If Rodchenko is unknown to Polonsky, that's not a fact of Rodchenko's life, but Polonsky's.

It is, of course, not right to blame me and my book *Third Factory*, which came out in 1926, for having influenced Rodchenko's letters written in 1925.

And it is unworthy of a Marxist, in general, to present the history of literature as though people are ruining each other.

The manner of publishing one's own letters during one's lifetime is an old one. Supplanting "artistic prose" with letters and memoirs is a common phenomenon in the history of literature.

It was Tolstoy, not Rozanov, who wrote that letters will supplant fiction.

Since the theater fireman who started singing by chance cannot be part of the troupe, he should neither be applauded nor reproached.

PROVISIONS I

Misapplying verbal clichés, a two-year-old says: "I lost the pencil with such great difficulty."

A delegation came to meet Yesenin's father, a peasant. He invited them into his hut. "Tell us about your son!" The old man crossed the room in his felt boots, sat down and began: "It was a dark night. It was raining, pouring like from a bucket …"

Receiving a thick manuscript, the editor of the publishing house asks:
　　"Is it a novel?"
　　"Yes, it's a novel."
　　"Is the heroine's name Nina?"
　　"Yes, Nina," the applicant gets excited.
　　"Take it back," says the editor sullenly.

Manuscripts written in different colored inks are not suitable for publication either.

Peasants are buying photographic cards at fairs and hanging them on the walls of their huts as decorations. Apparently, there is a lack of generals.

Many Russian prisoners roamed in Central Europe during the war. They went from Germany to Serbia, then to Turkey. Then they were caught in the revolution. It is hard to even imagine how the peasant has changed.

It was Gorky who taught Vsevolod Ivanov the Siberian language. He recorded five thousand words for Gorky. Not all the words have been used up. If anyone needs them, ask Vsevolod. He might give them away for free. He is a real writer.

I was comparing the 1927 Moscow edition of *L'Art poétique* with our *Poetics*, which was published in 1919. The paper has indeed gotten better!

The censor told an acquaintance of mine: "You have a style that's perfectly suitable for cutting."

A man, who was appointed as the head of a film studio, wrote the following note on the first script that he read (by Mikhail Levidov): "I read all night long. Didn't understand a thing. It's all in fragments. Rejected."

The editor, having read the works of a poet, said to him: "Your poems are splendid, but I won't publish them—I don't like them …" Then added pensively: "But you know, you somehow remind me of Bakunin."

A large publishing house circulated the following announcement: "The distribution of royalties is being suspended until further notice."

A young poet, who has just published his first chapbook, asks: "Do you think I will last in the history of literature?"

This is similar to when a woman of questionable repute asks: "Did I please you?"

A publisher (Uspensky) read a book that someone had given him, and said: "I haven't read anything in the past fifteen years. I read your book because I respect you very much. It's incomprehensible. Could you perhaps revise it?"

The writer did.

Vladimir Durov was telling: "I ordered walruses from abroad to teach them how to cut through mined fences."

"And were you able to?"

"No. I've only been able to teach them how to play on the guitar."

Pyotr Kogan used to wear a top hat in Paris, coming to exhibitions—it sat awkwardly on his head. That's how Lidia Seifullina wears her literary name today.

(I think) I saw a photograph of Konstantin Fedin. He was sitting at his desk between Tolstoy's and Gogol's busts.

He was sitting there—getting used to it.

FAIRY TALE PEOPLE

Fyodor Sologub has a fairy tale.

Once a girl and a boy went to the riverbank and saw a crayfish.

The crayfish walked on land, as they always do: going wherever the eyes go.

The children stood over it and shouted: "Look, the crayfish is moving backward!"

But the crayfish was moving forward, wherever his eyes wandered.

The children came running home and shouted: "Mama, we saw how a crayfish was walking backward, only it was a strange crayfish—his head and shoulders were in the back, and his tail was in the front!"

They are trying to persuade me that I am moving backward in cinematography.

It is assumed that if a studio is making films that are ideologically unsound, it must be the fault of an ideologically unsound person.

Or, according to the caricature in *Na postu* (*On Guard*), Shvedchikov is praying to the wrong person.[9]

---

9 Konstantin Shvedchikov, head of Sovkino, the State Committee for Cinematography.

In the meantime, I don't write only articles, but film scripts too. My scripts are read in workers' clubs and elsewhere. Apparently my head and everything else is in the right place.

But on the whole, it is possible to hold a conversation with the deaf.

Strange books have been appearing lately on bookstore shelves.

Dmitri Petrovsky, for example, is calling his recollections of Velimir Khlebnikov—a tale.

And the reader is reading Yuri Tynjanov's adapted version of Kyukhelbeker's biography and book about adventures as tales.

The facts are experienced aesthetically. A work of art today can also be without a plot.

One of the best books that Maksim Gorky wrote in recent years, among his other excellent works, is *Fragments from My Diary*.

What the artist considered to be draft material turned out to be his most artistic work.

Before they were extracting gold from the ore, now they are panning for radium.

It is especially worthwhile to write such a present-day tale about Velimir Khlebnikov.

Mayakovsky, Aseev, Pasternak, Tikhonov, and, of course, Petrovsky himself all have originated from Khlebnikov.

Even the most solid, the most traditional poets, such as Yesenin, were transformed by Khlebnikov's poetry.

He is a poet's poet. He is the Lomonosov of contemporary Russian literature. He is the vibration of the object: today's poetry is his sound.

The reader can't know him.

The reader will probably never hear him.

Touch Petrovsky's tales with your hand. You will feel the vibration.

Khlebnikov's destiny is more intelligible, easier to understand, than his poetry.

ON NATURE'S BEAUTY

Ivan Bunin's *Mitya's Love* is a result of the interaction of the Turgenevian genre and angst from Dostoevsky. The plot is taken from Tolstoy's *The Devil*. It is set in a Turgenevian landscape, rendered ever so monotonously. Here is the scheme of the landscape: sky, land, mood. This "trinity" recurs throughout the pages. The sky keeps getting darker and darker.

Verse is introduced for the conventional emphasis of banality and for discharging the possibility of parody.

The colors, as they say, are exquisite. Look them up in Dostoevsky's *Demons*; they are parodied in the description of a story called "Merci":

> Here the inevitable furze is growing all around (it is inevitably furze or some such plant, which has to be looked up in botany). At the same time there is inevitably some violet hue in the sky which, of course, no mortal has ever noticed—that is, everyone has seen it, but failed to notice it, "while I," he says, "I looked and am now describing it to you fools as a most ordinary thing." The tree under which the interesting couple sits is inevitably of some orange color.[10]

10   Fyodor Dostoevsky, *Demons*. Part Three, "The Fête. First Part," trans. Richard Pevear and Larissa Volokhonsky (New York: Alfred A. Knopf, 1994).

Bunin's descriptions stand in contradiction to each other:

> Looking down the row of adjoining rooms, he could see the library windows and a *pink*, motionless star suspended in the evening sky, which was such a constant shade of blue it seemed to have *no color* at all. Against that backdrop, the landscape seemed particularly picturesque, with the massive green crown of the ancient maple and all the *blossoms* in the garden, so white they made one think of *winter*. [11] [Emphasis mine—V.S.]

Here one often comes across things that are "colorless" and "beyond expression."

The bumblebees in Bunin are "velvety blackish-red," and that's because they have been painted over anew. He got that from Turgenev. Turgenev claimed that he could see things very clearly and even italicized the most striking words:

> It was she. But whether she was coming towards him, or going away from him, he could not be sure, until he saw that the patches of light and shadow glided *from below upwards* over her figure ... so she was approaching. They would have moved *from above downwards* if she had been walking away. [12]

Bunin's entire work is italicized. The descriptions are derived not from objects but from other descriptions. The landscape, in general, is a literary concept. It appeared and is experienced through tradition.

---

11   Ivan Bunin, *Mitya's Love* in *The Elagin Affair and Other Stories*, trans. Graham Hettlinger (Chicago: Ivan R. Dee, 2005).
12   Ivan Turgenev, *Virgin Soil*, trans. Constance Garnett (London: William Heinemann, 1920).

Pushkin's landscapes are archaic and consist of mentions of objects:

Dawn glowed in the east and golden ranks of clouds seemed to be awaiting the sun, like courtiers their sovereign.[13]

At last he reached a small glade, surrounded on all sides by the wood. A little stream ran silently among the trees, half of whose leaves had been blown off by the autumn winds. Vladimir stopped and sat down on the cold turf, and thoughts, each more gloomy than the last, oppressed his mind ... For a long time he sat motionless in the same place, watching the gentle flow of the stream as it carried away a few withered leaves, keenly struck by its similarity to life—a comparison which has become commonplace.[14]

The Volga flowed past the windows, carrying laden barges under full sail and small fishing-vessels, expressively called "soul-destroyers." Beyond the river hills and fields spread out into the distance and a few scattered villages gave life to the landscape. (*Dubrovsky*)

It is interesting to read the description of personal feelings by someone who has learned to appreciate the landscape. I am talking about the well-known memoirist—Andrei Bolotov.

He was born during the reign of Anna Ioannovna and died during the reign of Alexander I. He began writing his memoirs under the influence of *Gil Blas* and ended under the influence of Sterne.

This is how he learned about nature:

13   Aleksandr Pushkin, "The Lady Peasant" in *The Queen of Spades and Other Stories*, trans. Alan Myers (New York: Oxford University Press, 1997).
14   Aleksandr Pushkin, *Dubrovsky* in *The Complete Prose Tales*, trans. Gillon R. Aitken (New York: W. W. Norton, 1996).

Most fortuitously, I came across two books by the fine German author Johann Sulzer who wrote about the beauty of Nature. The subject matter contained in those books was completely new to me, but I was completely enraptured ... They acquainted me for the first time with the miraculous workings of the Universe and all the beauties of Nature. (Vol. I)

And by happy chance we rode up onto a hill from where all the lovely sights of places could be seen, as we were presented with a patterned view, and then I reasoned to consume it all with my eyes, thence using the moment for a special occasion to converse and to employ the sights for the purpose of probation, or, in plainer language, to check my companion's pulse from this end.

And pleased with what I saw, I began to speak as though to myself: "Ah! What a lovely sight of places and what pleasant scenes my eyes behold. What beautiful foliage! What different colors of fields! How remarkably the river curves and glistens, and how wonderfully does it correspond with the pure brilliance of the sky and those scattered little clouds." I spoke with deliberate sincerity, observing how my words fell on my companion's ear and what impression they made on him, and whether he remained the same unfeeling person, as it usually is with men of common stock ...

"What do I hear?" My companion rejoined. "Ah! How glad you have made me ... that I found in you what I had been looking for ... From a young age I had the fortune of being introduced to Nature and learning the precious art of comforting myself with all its beauties and graces." (Vol. III) [15]

15 Andrei Bolotov, *Zhizn i priklyuchenia Andreya Bolotova* [*The Life and Adventures of Andrei Bolotov*], 1789-1816.

This very same Bolotov built secluded mausoleums for himself during his lifetime, burying there his fallen teeth.

Ivan Bunin stands at the very end of this tradition.

He revives Turgenev's themes and devices with women's black underarms and material from Dostoevsky's dreams.

THE NAKED KING

When Aleksandr Blok's horse stumbled and fell, he managed to kick his feet out of the stirrups and jump off.

Larisa Reisner talked about him with fascination: "a real person." She was riding next to him.

Larisa Reisner herself was a real person—ravenous for life, a true friend, daring athlete, beautiful woman, inventive journalist. A person of long breath.

But "death doesn't know how to apologize."[16] Life lived halfway.

Reisner discovered herself as a writer in the newspaper.

Her feuilletons overloaded with images were outstanding.

She wrote as a true reporter. She never graced the paper with the work of a litterateur, but created a new genre out of journalism.

She had been in the Volga fleet battle, she had fought for Sviyazhsk, she had traversed the stone-ridden Afghanistan, the mines of Donbas and Kuznetsky reservoir, and the barricades of Hamburg.

Now Reisner wanted to fly to Tehran ... But her life was cut short.

16   From Vladimir Mayakovsky's "Vladimir Ilyich Lenin" (1924).

I remember Larisa Mikhailovna in Gorky's *Letopis* (*The Chronicle*). By the Peter and Paul Fortress during the February Revolution. At the Loskutnaya Hotel with the sailors. The revolution is a difficult thing for an intellectual. He is jealous of the revolution, as a husband would be jealous of his wife. Doesn't recognize her. Fears her.

It is easier to acknowledge a revolution aesthetically when she is weak.

It was as difficult for the writer, the student of the Symbolists, the friend of the Acmeists Larisa Reisner to go through the daily grind and victories of the revolution as it was for the destroyers under Raskolnikov's command that had to pass through the Mariinsk Canal System to the Caspian Sea.

Few of us can boast that we have seen the revolution not through a vent window. People from the old literary culture were able to accept the February Revolution and the first days of the October Revolution, but Larisa had the spirit and faith for traveling all the way to Afghanistan and Hamburg.

We will remember our friend for a long time. Larisa Mikhailovna was better at telling than writing—more ironic and less ornate.

She was telling how at a memorial service, in Hamburg, they played a requiem or funeral march on mandolins and cried in one room, while others danced to the music in the adjacent room.

And about a poor unemployed man who was given a top hat by his friends, so he could bury his wife with honor.

It is important to talk about such things, so that one can anticipate the waiting period.

Some two months ago, Larisa Mikhailovna told me the following about cinema in the East. She was going to write about it:

The houses of the whites are secluded. The white man in the East has a clean-shaven face, clean as a signboard. The color compels.

And in the corner sits Nikolai Tikhonov's "Sami" and watches.

The white man stands his ground.

And then cinematography arrives. Cheap, tattered, like the ones in our clubs, films are shown in Persia, India, Polynesia.

Conrad Veidt and Charlie Chaplin hosted by Africans and Indians.

It turns out:

The white man is a thief. His wife cheats on him. The white master cries. He is beaten. The white master is a liar.

Now when the Sahib walks in the street, colored people know that the king is naked.

And he is not even clean.

Cinema with bourgeois themes in the East is a perlustration of the masters' mail.

The Indian governors are in shock. They are demanding a re-montage of films.

They are banning cinematography.

That's how the Austrian generals, after they won the revolution, destroyed the streetlamps in Naples.

There is a cheerfulness of faith in the objective truth of life in this story.

Electricity, cinema, and even plumbing cannot not be our allies.

This was the least I could do for a friend: preserve a piece of something that she didn't have the time to write down.

IN DEFENSE OF THE
SOCIOLOGICAL METHOD[17]

The writer manipulates the contradictory perspectives in his work, which he doesn't always create. Perspectives and their alternation are often created not by the same genetics of formal moments. The writer makes use of devices that have different origins. He sees their conflict. Changes the functions of the devices. Applies a device to another kind of material. That is how Derzhavin developed the ode with the low style.[18] While Gogol transferred song devices onto themes originally connected with Ukraine, but qualitatively assessed in a different way, and then onto themes not connected with Ukraine.

That's the genesis of one of the devices of Gogolian humor.

17   Footnote by V. Shklovsky—From a lecture, presented in Leningrad on March 6, 1927.
18   According to Mikhail Lomonosov, the Russian vernacular and Church Slavonic could be combined in three styles, depending on the writer's goals: the first, "high" style, used for tragedies, odes, and elegies, would include more Slavonicisms; the second, "middle" style, used for drama, elegy, and satire, would consist of an equal mix of Russian vernacular and Church Slavonic; and the third, "low" style, used for comedies, epigrams, songs, and everyday speech, would incorporate mostly the Russian vernacular.

EXCURSUS

As to what concerns Comrade Pereverzev's discovery, that the nature around the estates of small landowners is poorer than the nature around the estates of large landowners, it is dead wrong. In fact, it is worth it to quote from his book *Tvorchestvo Gogolya* [*The Art of Gogol*, 1914]: "There cannot be any doubt that the nature around a city or a small estate is poorer than the nature around a large estate."

And yet I doubt it. Landowners practiced intermingled strip farming in Russia.

In any case, Pereverzev, being a knowledgeable man and not one of those graduates who read lectures on literary history in higher educational institutions, is working with poor-quality material.

For example, he ascribes Gogol to the class of small landowners and transfers the relations of Russian serfdom onto Ukraine without a reservation. Meanwhile:

> When creating the lists of electors from the Slobodsko-Ukrainian province for Catherine's Commission they found out that there were no noblemen in the precise meaning of the word in the province among the local residents. Instead, there were owners of settled and unsettled lands who came from the ranks of regimental and squadron seniority.[19]

The nobility in Ukraine is very young.

In the next pages Pereverzev unreservedly conflates the nobility with government officials. Whereas during Catherine's reign,

---

19   Grigori Meerson, *Rannyaya burzhuaznaya revolyutsia v Rossii* [*Early Bourgeois Revolution in Russia*], 1925.

"The class of functionaries and government officials was even smaller in number and was definitely made up of common people."[20]

During Paul's reign, noblemen were forbidden to take civil service jobs (to bypass this regulation they tried to create a special Senate Regiment). And noblemen started taking up positions in civil service only at the end of Alexander's reign and at the beginning of Nicholas's reign.

Eugene in *The Bronze Horseman* is a hereditary, not a ranked nobleman. He is an outcast.

And the natural economy is not typical for the Catherine period. The Skotinins in *The Minor* breed pigs for exporting lard. Korobochka in *Dead Souls* deals in procurement.

There possibly was a return to the "naturalization" of economy during the reign of Nicholas. (In 1825 the price for bread in the world decreased by sixty-five percent.) One ought to study these facts and not simply search for their reflection in literature.

Lev Tolstoy, by the way, whom Pereverzev considers a member of the gentry, was in fact a small landowner and in his letters to Fet called one hundred desyatins[21] a large estate.

HOW ONE SHOULDN'T WORK

This whole business of drawing facts from literature, which are then checked in history books, is not scientific at all, as it does not take into account the laws of deformation. And besides, this method belongs to an intensive movement of a vicious cycle.

---

20   From Aleksandr Pushkin's annotations to the eighth chapter of *The History of Pugachov's Revolt* (1834).

21   An old Russian unit of land area measurement equal to approximately 2.7 acres.

Pereverzev's indications that Gogol easily translated the subject matter from a landowner's social reality to a functionary's prove the dysfunctionality of the link between social realities and their "reflections" (an absolutely harmful term). That's also how a device is transferred from the Spanish culture to the Russian. That's how Goncharov, using a merchant's way of life, portrayed the village of Oblomovka.

THE CRUSADERS

During their first crusades, they mistook each city for Jerusalem. When, upon entering the city, they would find out that it was not Jerusalem, they would destroy it.

Out of disappointment.

Meanwhile, Jerusalem exists.

FACTS MEANWHILE DO EXIST

At the same time, the Formalists (OPOYAZ) do not want to oppose the scientific fact.

If facts are destroying the theory, then that's best for the theory.

It was created by us, and not handed over to us for preservation.

The change of aesthetic material is a social fact—let's trace it in *The Captain's Daughter*.

THE CAPTAIN'S DAUGHTER

Comrade Voronsky is a disillusioned man and a libertarian. He has doubts about Jerusalem.

When analyzing *The Captain's Daughter*, he found out that the "hare skin jacket" was a classless fact, as though Pushkin had stopped being a nobleman here.

Voronsky evidently was trying to prove with this jacket that *The Captain's Daughter* can still be read today.

Let's try to make sense of this.

The Captain's Daughter is made of three quoted themes:

1. An outlaw who offers help.

The outlaw has the same function as the helping animal in folk tales. The hero offers him some kind of service, and later the outlaw, in turn, saves him. It is an old theme that survives the centuries because it helps untangle plot impediments. This theme is still alive today in the historical novel (Sienkiewicz's *With Fire and Sword*, Khmelnitsky and Skrzetuski; Conan Doyle, etc.). It must have reached Pushkin through Walter Scott's *Rob Roy*. The whole structure of the novel—supposedly not written but simply published by Pushkin, who divided it into chapters and furnished it with epigraphs—is entirely a Walter-Scottian device.

So the "classless" in *The Captain's Daughter* is the aesthetical, the referential. The image of the noble and grateful outlaw, as well as his two assistants—"the villain" and the "nonvillain"—all of this is tradition.

The classlessness is beyond the artist's will.

2. Grinyov, not wanting to implicate Masha, does not testify.

This is another borrowed device. The impossibility to testify or the impossibility to speak until a certain time can be found in fairy tales and their variations, for instance, "The Seven Viziers," the German fairy tales. In novels, as in fairy tales, this is a retardation device. Only the motive has changed.

3. The second point is resolved when the woman talks about herself.

The theme of Masha's meeting with Empress Catherine is evidently taken simultaneously from *The Heart of Midlothian* and *Parasha, the Siberian Girl*.

I am deliberately sidestepping the original outline of *The Captain's Daughter*. Initially Grinyov and Shvabrin were the same person, and the whole story was based on the pardon of the noble outlaw.

But the versions that were not included in the book are principally different from what the author did publish and can bring us closer to the psychology of the creative process.

So what is class-based in *The Captain's Daughter*?

First and foremost, the perversion of history.

The fortress of Belogorsk is actually the fortress of Chernoretsk.

But historic Orenburg had a rampart that encompassed an area of five and a half versts.[22] It had stone walls, a hundred cannons, twelve Howitzers, and an army of over four thousand men.

It was a first-rate fortress (though not completely finished).

There were, of course, more than thirty men in the fortress of Belogorsk, somewhere between two hundred and thirty and three hundred and sixty soldiers, not counting the Cossacks.

Mironov was supposed to be a large landowner.

Let me quote from Captain-Lieutenant Savva Mavrin's report to Catherine: "... When the service people in the provinces are mostly plowmen, what else can they do in the fortresses of

---

22   An old Russian unit of length equal to about 2/3 of a mile.

Sorochinsk, Tatishchev, Sakmara, and elsewhere but trade? And they are not to blame, as all the commanders in those places have their own houses and live as landowners, while they are all their tributaries."[23]

The Belogorsk idyll was a sham, and Pushkin knew it. He also knew that the historical Palashka complained to Pugachov in the fortress of Chernoretsk about her barin (the commandant).

The Orenburg steppe was not a wasteland. There were big trading towns there. I am not talking about Orenburg. Around fifteen thousand people lived in Yaitsk. Trade caravans passed through. There were salt mines there.

Something to fight for.

Pushkin, while working on the historical material, did the following. He wrote in the annotations not what had happened in history, and history does not contain anything that is in *The Captain's Daughter*.

He wanted to show the rebellion as being brutal and pointless and that's why he created the Belogorsk idyll and stripped the fortress of all its reality. Nothing is real there except for the snow and Grinyov.

The fortress has been weakened (he describes the outpost, instead of the fortress) so that the adversary doesn't appear too strong. The log walls of the Tatishchev fortress shouldn't surprise us, as the Turkish fortress of Ismail in Byron's *Don Juan* also had log palisades.

The outlaw, who arranges weddings, brings us back, of course, into the conventional world.

One of the more interesting characters in the Belogorsk fortress is Father Gerasim.

---

23   Nikolai Dubrovin, *Pugachov i yego soobshchniki* [*Pugachov and His Accomplices*], 1884.

As you know, the clergy would meet Pugachov with a cross. Later the synod wrote a great deal about this.

In Pushkin, Father Gerasim also meets Pugachov with a cross. But Pushkin alters the motivation in a brilliant way: "Father Gerasim, pale and trembling, was standing by the steps with a cross in his hands and seemed to be silently imploring mercy for future victims."[24]

Historically Savelyich was supposed to join the rebels.

Pushkin understands this.

But Savelyich is "a loyal folk." So Pushkin splits his character (a common device today) and projects it onto Vanka.

We meet Vanka on the floating gallows: "It was our servant Vanka—poor Vanka, who, in his foolishness, went over to Pugachov."

Before this scene Vanka has so few lines (I am certain the reader doesn't even remember him) that we can assume Vanka was inserted for historical verisimilitude. He substitutes Savelyich.

Pushkin is not always successful in hiding history. For example, it is not clear what kind of "passport" the rebelling peasants are demanding to see. Pugachovian, I suppose.

But without establishing, organizing a Pugachovian state, Pushkin simply didn't motivate the "passport" and used it as a sign of the rebellion's illogicality. The "cavalry raids" in which Grinyov is secretly taking part are also not developed. The nobility's partisanship was typical of those times.

Pushkin couldn't show it because then he would have to expose the rear of Pugachov's army.

Ideologically speaking, *The Captain's Daughter* is an ingenious and brilliantly well-balanced (ideologically sound) work. The aesthetic clichés made the work acceptable even for the other classes.

24   Pushkin, *The Captain's Daughter*, trans. Natalie Duddington (London: J. M. Dent, 1961).

THE FURTHER FATE OF THE WORK

With time, *The Captain's Daughter* is becoming aestheticized. Its situations are (very quickly) losing their original setup. They are turning into pure aesthetic material. Pushkin's Orenburg steppe emerges. The aestheticized material, which from the very beginning included in itself purely formal moments, becomes crystallized.

When it was the anniversary of Pugachov's rebellion, they nonchalantly decided to bring out a deluxe edition of *The Captain's Daughter*.

The Bashkirs, who were beyond our aesthetic habits, protested.

But the work has really lost its original meaning. It got separated from its intention.

Placed next to the aesthetic material, the historical material becomes something else for the reader, not what Pushkin had intended to write.

A pamphlet becomes successful precisely when it is used outside the scope of its original purpose. Osip Brik's unpublished analysis of the first and second editions of *Fathers and Sons* is an excellent example of such a phenomenon.

The original meaning is often revived in the attempt to transfer the work onto a different material.

CONCERNING PUSHKIN

We treat Pushkin from the standpoint of production.

As a technician treats another technician.

If he were alive (he would be different), we would have to vote whether to admit him in *Novy LEF* (*New LEF*) or not.

Then we would try to get him into the Federation of Writers. They would ask us: "How many writers does Comrade Pushkin represent?"

My imagination abandons me here.

But still, what does Pushkin's name mean today?

I will quote from Lev Voitolovsky's *History of Russian Literature* (1926): "It is the literature of the nobility that reproduces to the minutest detail the livelihood and morals of the Russian gentry of that period. Onegin, Lensky, Hermann, Prince Yeletsky, Tomsky, Gremin … In their image, Pushkin gives …"

Let me inform the much-acclaimed scholar Voitolovsky that the characters he is listing here are baritone and tenor roles of an opera. Gremin, Tatyana's husband (?) who sings the aria "All ages are to love submissive," doesn't exist in Pushkin.

It is not commendable to study Russian literature (sociologically) through opera.

A SOUL OF DOUBLE WIDTH

Our writers have a dual soul. Or, at least, that is what the critics are saying. They cannot find unity of style in the writer.

Here is an excerpt from Ivan Grevs's new book *Istoria odnoi lyubvi* (*A Story of a Love Affair*, 1927):

> Finally Turgenev—awaiting fearfully for Pauline Viardot's verdict, in a very decisive, unpleasantly blunt style to which unfortunately he resorts every so often in conversations and personal correspondence, and which acutely contrasts the elegance of his true literary language—offers his own, definitely unfair characterization of his original story "A Lear of the Steppes" to Ludwig Pietsch (April 16, 1870): "I have finished the story. In its crudeness it reminds me of large buttocks, not Rubenesque, of course—with rosy cheeks, but very ordinary, fat, pale Russian buttocks."

How obscenely long is Grevs's comment!

What a confusing sentence!

And it's ungrammatical. This is how professors write. We can find a vocabulary of forbidden words in Tolstoy too (for instance, his comparison of poetry and prose with rectal parts). It's not a matter of the writer's personality here. Tolstoy and Turgenev aren't alike. It's two different traditions stipulating the style of literature and personal letter.

This is how the Russian aristocracy spoke Russian sometimes deliberately using the vernacular.

Genres are chosen. Not two souls, but several genres. The structure of the soul in literature is moderated. You can play on blacks, but you will lose a quarter of shades ... All of this constricts the notion of literature as an utterance of the soul even more.

Literary genres exist in the writer as the properties of a black rabbit in a white rabbit born from a black and white one.

Shave its fur in the winter frost. It will grow back black hair.

Zavadovsky does the same in zoology.

Climate change is a nonliterary fact.

"The reaction of the organism to external stimuli—cold, in this case—is entirely determined by the hereditary ability of the animal, the inner strength that it has inherited."

Veselovsky sometimes came close to this idea.

WHERE GORKY IS GOING

The Life of Klim Samgin does not adhere to anything. It's just belletristic prose that just gets published. It is an impossible work, like a building that cannot stand.

One must have some sort of innate respect for great literature and complete disregard for technique to publish writers like that.

They are catching catfish from one installment to the next. We learn about Feng Yuxiang's betrayal, important events are taking place in Wuhan, there is a revolution in Vienna, and they are still trying to catch catfish in *Klim Samgin*. The non-coincidence of the novel's pace with the pace of the newspaper where it's being published is extremely comical. Is it possible that someone who has read about the events in Vienna or about other such events would ever ask: "What about the catfish? Did they catch it?" They didn't, and anyway, it turned out that the peasants were deceiving the intelligentsia.

I am not against Gorky's novel, although Gorky, along with a group of other writers who are, generally speaking, beginners, is now a victim of the focus on great literature. But if I were to object to the catfish, per se, I could say that it is directly derived from the lynx in Balzac's *The Peasantry*. There, too, people were trying to catch a nonexistent lynx, which the peasants used for deceiving the intelligentsia.

So the catfish, swimming in the pages of the newspaper, is a quoted catfish.

Gorky is a well-read depicter of everyday life (*bytovik*).

ANDREI BELY

Andrei Bely walks around Tiflis holding a black umbrella behind his back—the only umbrella in the city. It is around thirty degrees Celsius in the shade and there is not a hint of rain in the sky. People in Tiflis don't walk in the streets after four o'clock, and basically stand around all dressed in white and don't go anywhere. They stand like this during the day and they stand like this after it gets dark. Bely walks among them wearing a panama hat on his gray head and holding his black umbrella.

Those who carry black umbrellas in Georgia and Adjara aside from him are the shepherds and contrabandists. The shepherds normally carry umbrellas because the sun is too bright.

But you shouldn't look indiscriminately at everything in the world; you will stumble upon the same thing in the end. The meadows in the Caucasian mountains are the same as the meadows in the Alps and the Carpathians, and the shepherds in the Carpathians have the same black umbrellas, and the stone roofs in Adjara are the same as in Switzerland. These are two different places on the same floor, and while observing the world we often end up acting like people on a film expedition organized by Goskino,[25] who were driving to Siberia in a parallel circle and getting surprised that the nature along the Lena River is the same as the nature south of Moscow.

ON GENRES

I wrote earlier about the double soul of the artist. I need to explain what I mean by this.

My point is that the writer belongs simultaneously to several literary traditions, rather than have a double soul. In the same way, a person born to parents who are psychologically very different is subject to his maternal and paternal lines alternately. Mixing a black rabbit with a white rabbit won't make a gray rabbit, but a rabbit with white and black patches.

And the writer also belongs simultaneously to several literary genres. Gogol didn't experience a splitting of his soul when he began corresponding with his friend; he simply wished to include in the correspondence his old material from *Arabesques*—he continued a different line.

Rousseau said that *Julie, or the New Héloïse* would not have been published at a different time and regretted not having lived in that period.

---

25   The State Committee for Cinematography.

39

Using this analogy, I will quickly say the following regarding genres: there cannot be an *arbitrary* number of literary systems. Just as chemical elements do not join randomly to form compounds, but only join in a specific ratio according to their masses, just as there are no random kinds of rye but only known formulas of rye that produce a specific kind of rye, or just as there are no random amounts of crude oil and only, perhaps, a fixed amount, so there is a specific number of literary genres based on a specific crystallography of literary plots.

They are complicated by materializing in various types of material, and the value of their own material is different; sometimes they even transfer to the field of colloidal chemistry and are purely focused on the material.

EXTRACT

In order to simplify the polemic, I will state my objections to Comrade Pereverzev, apologizing to him in advance, as my objections are shorter than his book and, therefore, formulated less precisely.

FIRST GENERAL OBJECTION

Since literary works change in their technique rather quickly and, in any case, undergo serious changes within a few years, one must—when examining the influence from a social basis— study that basis using the same scale, i.e., using the same degree of divisibility that would correlate to the real changes of the literary material.

SECOND GENERAL OBJECTION

If we are going to call anything that happens in society "social," then, of course, literary borrowing is a social phenomenon. But the fact that a particular literary phenomenon may survive the social conditions that created it is a special kind of social fact. And genre has to be studied in its specific conditions.

THIRD OBJECTION OF A SPECIFIC KIND

Comrade Pereverzev's claim that in the 1830s the nobility was just getting used to currency and that they were experiencing a period of transition from the natural to the monetary economy is simply not accurate. Taking the scale of literary changes into consideration, I find the assertion that Gogol (a nobleman who easily agreed on being transferred from the sixth book to the eighth book)[26] was simply a "nobleman" to be so unspecific that it cannot be used for any kind of analysis.

FOURTH OBJECTION OF A SPECIFIC KIND

I think it is possible to refute Comrade Pereverzev's argument that the brass candleholder on Manilov's dandyish table is a fact that directly exposes Manilov's social position by arguing that the introduction of the candleholder is a simple comical device, and the material here, consequently, appears in a deformed state.

All of my arguments above lead to the conclusion that the work of my colleagues who are using the sociological method is too general and it cannot fully evaluate the specificity of the material.

---

26   Gogol wrote to his mother in February 1849, regarding a delicate matter where she had to prove her nobility: "But do not feel too alarmed by this. All of it is utter nonsense. Having a piece of bread is more important, than whether one is of ancient nobility or common nobility, or whether one is registered in the *sixth* book or the *eighth*."

In regards to our future work, in particular the work on the history of literary royalties and print runs of books, we are not claiming that it will resolve the question on the relationship of literary and nonliterary systems. But it is work that needs to be done. It is important to introduce new facts into our consciousness. So I ask colleagues not to reprimand us for doing the work that they themselves didn't do, evidently due to a lack of time, which was partially spent on the creation of chrestomathies and other science popularization work.

PROVISIONS II

Gorky argued with a top Communist official around the question: Do people understand Marx's statement that "religion is the opium of the masses"?

They decided to ask a Red Army guard.

"What's opium?"

"I know," he said, "it's a medicine."

Perhaps this is why religion by the Iberian Gate is not *opium* anymore but *Devil's snare.*

When they write about newspaper language, they infinitely simplify the matter by citing examples where readers have misunderstood certain words.

But that's not the issue here.

Opium really *is* a medicine.

The issue is not that people don't understand the word, but that they don't know its narrow meaning.

I am not talking about replacing the word with another one, but imparting the reader with as much knowledge as possible. The word exists in a phrase. We need dictionaries of concepts, not dictionaries of words.

It doesn't matter if they are Russian words or foreign words.

In the meantime we are interested in translation—that's good.

But it turned out that the journalists were using words they didn't understand. Take, for instance, Yakov Shafir's dictionaries. Everything there is inaccurate.

The word "champion" was translated as "instigator" in one of the major newspapers of the capital.

Shafir was one of the instigators of the incident. And he is also the champion of imprecise meanings.

One must know his words. The word *khaltura*, for example. Where does it come from?[27]

Some say that it is derived from the Greek word *chalkos*—bronze.

The clergy differentiated two kinds of income: parochial and *khalturial*. In the south of Russia the latter meant the payment for certain sacerdotal services (for a private party) performed outside of one's eparchy.

The word migrated from the church singers to the orchestrants. In 1918-19 the word began to spread like rats during Catherine's reign and, carried by the actors and performers, it took over the whole country.

Gorky assures that the word *kholt* in Kazan means an object that doesn't correspond to its signifier. For example, a soap that doesn't lather. It turns out, then, that the word *khaltura* is derived from the Kazan Tatar language.

Roshchin-Grossman, Polonsky, Sakulin, and someone else are always proposing a synthesis. They keep telling me I need to

---

27 Shklovsky uses the verb *iskhalturitsa* (derived from the root word *khaltura*) in the preface, where he explains the concept of the Hamburg score: "It is a long, hard, and ugly fight. But this is the only way to determine their true worth—to prevent them from getting corrupted (*iskhalturitsa*)."

marry the formal method to something else. The children, they say, will be phenomenal.

There are two kinds of *khaltura*: Greek and Tatar.

Greek *khaltura* is when a person writes in a place where he is not supposed to write and sings where he is not supposed to sing.

Tatar *khaltura* is when a person doesn't work as he is supposed to.

The representatives of each group despise one another and are in eternal enmity.

Today this enmity has evolved into a fight between the "fellow travelers" and "on-guardists."[28]

28   The *poputchiks* or "fellow travelers" were the writers and artists sympathetic to the goals of the October Revolution, but who declined to join the Communist Party. The term was first introduced by Lev Trotsky in the second chapter of his book *Literature and Revolution* (1924, trans. Rose Strunsky):

> Between bourgeois art, which is wasting away either in repetitions or in silences, and the new art, which is yet unborn, there is being created a transitional art that is more or less organically connected with the Revolution, but that is not at the same time the art of the Revolution. Boris Pilnyak, Vsevolod Ivanov, Nikolai Tikhonov, the "Serapion Brotherhood," Yesenin and his group of Imagists and, to some extent, Klyuev—all of them were impossible without the Revolution, either as a group, or separately ... They are not the artists of the proletarian Revolution, but her artist "fellow travelers," in the sense in which this word was used by the old Socialists.

Later, however the "fellow travelers" (along with the writers of *LEF* and *New LEF*) were attacked as counterrevolutionaries by members of the Moscow Association of Proletarian Writers (MAPP) who had launched the critical journal *Na postu* (*On Guard*, 1923-5), and who were known as the "on-guardists." The "on-guardists" demanded the centralization of literary life and strict control over the "fellow travelers." The editorial staff included Semyon Rodov, Grigori Lelevich (Labori Kalmanson), Ilya Vardin (Illarion Mgeladze), Boris Volin, and Leopold Averbakh. In 1926 *Na postu* was renamed *Na literaturnom postu* (*On Literary Guard*) and was published until 1932.

The trump card of the first group of *khalturshchiks* is talent, while the trump card of the second group of *khalturshchiks* is the rightness of their direction. There are also mixed, Greek-Tatar types.

Art exists separately.

According to the scriptwriter Georgi Grebner, who has just returned from the Votsk Republic, Christianity among the Votians died off immediately after the fall of the Romanov Dynasty, but the pagan priests are still around. They are like agronomists: they give advice on how to manage the economy, while at the same time make sacrifices and slaughter black cattle in fir groves. We don't see the worship of gods in the southern parts of Votsk, and yet all Votians have a special small house in their yard, which has a cupboard where they place bread and vodka (*kumyshka*). In the North, they paint a goose on the cupboard. The goose is the god of water. The starling is the god of air. Occasionally they elect a fourteen-year-old male virgin as their priest.

But on the whole, virginity is not respected there.

The Votians are conducting ethnographic excavations now in search of their history, and a former woman priest was nominated as a candidate to the Central Executive Committee. When a woman dies, they slaughter a cow (it doesn't have to be black). When a man dies, they slaughter a horse. When they need to expel the devil out of a house, they hit the house with a log (and Votian houses are big, two-storied houses). The devil is thus shaken out of the house, and driven out of the village. Cinematographers don't go there, but photographers occasionally do.

Fyodorovich is astonishingly eloquent in the newspaper *Pravda* (*Truth*). When he writes about Turkestan, he presents it with such exoticism that it seems you are not reading a newspaper but watching a film by Dmitri Bassalygo. But it's too bad that Fyodorovich doesn't use a map or an encyclopedic dictionary when writing his articles. Then he would know that pendinka is not a venereal disease, and that he is making revolutionary, heroic women in the steppes, where the railroad passes, flee from the parasites at two to three hundred versts on horseback. One shouldn't be so eloquent in a newspaper.

Such things happen here, because when they want to praise a journalist, they tell him: "What a journalist! Not even a journalist, an outright belletrist!" And they think they are elevating him to a higher rank by saying this.

If you need a writer for a scientific expedition, who rides his horse with patience, who is not afraid of the heat, and who won't tell anyone what is going on in his stomach if he has eaten something that can't be found in the encyclopedia. If you need such a writer, contact our editorial staff at *New LEF* and we will send you someone. We are willing to relocate. We don't care about distance.

One of my acquaintances, a young writer, worked as a shepherd in a village before becoming a writer. He was a Komsomol member and wanted to revolutionize the village, but the *kulaks*[29] decided to kill him. The shepherd wandered from house to house

29 Wealthy landed peasants in tsarist Russia, characterized by the Communists during the October Revolution as exploiters.

like a travel journalist who writes about landmarks and the construction of power stations. The shepherd would spend the night in someone's house for one sheep; one cow was worth two sheep. They tortured the shepherd using various methods: they used an axe on him and forced him to drink acid. But somehow he would always survive and go out into the street each morning to play his horn. The villagers would wake up and say drowsily: "He's still alive!" Now he is in Moscow and wants to apply to the State Institute of Cinematography.

They beat the writer Svetozarov in one village, as he was traveling on a boat alone from Moscow to Astrakhan, but the children in that same village knew the poems of Vasili Kazin by heart.

When someone writes a script for a comedy, everyone tries a hand at changing it. By the way, this is how they determine a driver's level of inexperience. Suppose there is a car. Sery approaches the car and sounds the car horn—this signals that he is an inept driver. Syroi approaches the car and starts changing the gears, which breaks the car.[30] The filmscript is altered by both "gray" and "damp" people. They all want to show how smart they are if they work for the Commissariat of Enlightenment. First they sound the horn, play with the headings, then they think of themselves as artistic individuals, quasi-drivers, and change a whole episode. Only a very cultured and self-restrained person can stop himself from poking a finger, from altering something.

---

30 *Sery* and *syroi* are adjectives in Russian, meaning "gray" and "damp" respectively.

I remember how during a film screening the wife of the factory
director pondered for a while and then said with an inspired
voice: "Wouldn't it be great if we added an intertitle here that
said: *And in the meantime?*" As a result, our scripts don't turn
out to be as funny as they should be. Stop working on someone
else's workstation!

Chaliapin would say: "Such and such actor keeps coming to my
performances. Do you think he's coming to learn something?
He's been waiting for a decade now for me to lose my voice." This
is so characteristic of our mores. Pushkin said: "We are lazy and
not curious."[31] Do you remember on what occasion he said this?
He was commenting on the absence of Griboedov's biography.
We, the Formalists, are curious and we aren't lazy, and Tynjanov
wrote Griboedov's biography. Our friends have been sitting in
the audience for a decade now, waiting for us to lose our voices,
meanwhile they are suppressing us in the paper.

I split ways with a driver in 1917. He was a Bolshevik, a good
driver who used to be a lathe operator—a driver from the worker
ranks. It was very difficult to get along with him, as we were
very different. Six years later I was approached by a man with a
familiar voice at a car rally, and it should be said that it's nearly
impossible to recognize a person wearing a helmet—you can
only see the nose, eyebrows, and the mouth. He said his name:
it was the same driver. "I'm writing now," I told him. "You don't
have to tell me, I follow what goes on in literature," he said in

31   From "A Journey to Arzrum" (1836).

an offended voice. The man had learned a lot. I don't know if he had lost his former venomousness during this period.

With great difficulty the writer wrenches his verbal composition out of the automatism of the habitual day. The work of the writer becomes a habitual transition into a new aesthetic sphere—the aesthetic of clichés.

They write new biographies, according to this new perception. More precisely, the biography replaces the anecdote.

The monuments by the great tombs are inscribed with the best wishes of the philistines. They bestow upon the dead their own virtues.

There is a film by Vladimir Gardin called *The Poet and the Tsar* (1927). Two parts of the film are engaged with fountains. The real title, therefore, should have been "The Poet and the Fountains."

In the film, Pushkin is endowed with youth, which he didn't have before his death, beauty, and ideological soundness.

He reads folk poems to the peasants. He despises Nicholas. At home he sits down and writes poems. Right in front of the public's eyes.

He sits down by the table.

He sits for a while like that, then gets up and reads: "I've raised a monument to myself not wrought by hands."[32]

In a domestic setting, before Gardin, Pushkin used to say that one could still eat at a restaurant, even if one had a house cook. But now he has changed. He stays at home, loves only his wife, and lets the children ride on his back.

---

32   The first line of Pushkin's "Exegi Monumentum" (1836).

It's impossible to understand the real Pushkin, apparently.

They had to turn him into a dummy.

When he is killed, they put him in a box and send him with a Feldjäger officer to be buried in a village.

The set director attaches lanterns to the carriage. It looks beautiful, but it doesn't convey the meaning of transporting the corpse in a box, of robbing the dead man of his fame.

The pavilions are huge, and the masquerade, the different masks are apparently supposed to portray Pushkin's soul. Pushkin died somewhere on the outskirts of the city. When they found his papers, his friends were astonished: "Pushkin thought. Pushkin was a thinker!"

Bulgarin is portrayed in an episode as a villain, of course. He goes around buying up Sovremennik. Then there is Gogol listening to the recital of poems. There is no use in talking about chronology. The only historically accurate item in the film is probably Pushkin's robe. All of this reminds me of an illustration for learning a foreign language: they are reaping in the first corner, sowing in the second, there is a fire in the third, and they are plowing in the fourth. Even if there was no snow, they would have created it for the film.

They installed another monument on Strastnaya Square in honor of these fountains.

The painting on canvas depicts a winter scene, like in the photographs. Against it—a young man with long straight legs and fur on his head, the "dummy" of d'Anthès, and the dummy of Pushkin in an oilcloth cape. The edges of their eyes are painted blue.

All this is illiterate nonsense—the rash of the disease afflicting cinematography.

The financial inspector came to Buryatia and sent out tax forms to the city dwellers. He woke up in the morning, came out of his tent. There was no sign of the city. The city had left at night. People say they saw it (the city) about a hundred versts away.

Now imagine the peasant from the Red Army during the Civil War; the peasant who was a war prisoner in Germany and was newly demobilized, and for whom they read widely in the barracks, read even from culinary books. There are three kinds of demobilized peasants in the village (they own ten percent of our literary themes).

I met with a former Red Army commander at his dacha in the village. There was an engraved Mauser on the wall of the poor hut.

The demobilized commander was leasing a ferryboat jointly with the peasants. He had a contusion and was feverish.

"They had mills," he said to me, "they had mills, which I destroyed ..." By "they" he meant the former Whites who were now converted peasants. One of them was even captured and imprisoned by the Germans. There were photographs on the wall of his hut depicting students in uniform.

The family had left the village, but they were forced back into peasantry by the revolution.

"Can you tell me how much I can own and not be considered a kulak?" the short host asked me.

So the people living in the village are quite diverse.

And a peasant, afraid to go over the limit in his household, was plowing with calves—not out of poverty, but out of
conspiracy.

The calves (they were called "pioneers") are not counted as
draft animals. Cows are also used for plowing, though they end
up with less milk because of that.

Cities can be strange too.

There is no tea in Boguchar, not even one-eighth of a pound.
Nobody is rich in tea. The residents of the city are mostly carriage drivers. And the only form of entertainment is radio. In the
meantime, they have already built the water pipeline of the city.

We don't know anything about our villages.

A university student from the village, a quiet young man with
thick, unruly, white hair was telling me the following.

An old peasant woman and her son were cutting grass in the
Olonets province, far away from the village, behind the mud
grounds. In the morning, the mother asked her son: "Is it true
that there is no God?" The son probably said yes.

"It would've been good if there was none," the mother sighed.

The remarkable thing here is the reality of yearning and wish
for "no God."

He gets in the way.

LITERATURE

TEN YEARS

We have forgotten many things since then. We have lost many things. We have lost, for example, the footage from the first Bolshevik May Day, shot by Lev Kuleshov.

The years have produced clichéd recollections. The clichés melded with memory and became heroicized.

It is very difficult for a writer to overcome his own manner of writing and to remember. Here is what I remember.

There were slender big-leaf aspens growing in the factory yards. The birches had already spread to the ruins of the County Courthouse. Very beautiful walls. The grass had covered Manezhny Lane. The houses stood with closed mouths—the front entrances.

The Neva was light blue in the summer. People swam in the pond of the Summer Garden. They played *ryukhi*[33] by the atlantes on the portico of the Hermitage.

They plowed with wooden plows behind a rusty iron sheet fence on the corner of Kronverksky Prospect and Vvedenskaya

---

33   An old Russian game, also known as *gorodki*, the object of which is to throw a wooden bat at sets of blocks arranged in various formations inside a demarcated area— the *gorod* or city. The goal is to knock these formations out of the "city" in as few throws as possible.

Street. The bridges and the city stood as an unreconstructed fortress of iron. The sky was clear and smoke-free.

There was a long, unremitting line of people along the Moika embankment waiting to get permission to leave the country. They were putting their fingerprints on the documents.

Merezhkovsky sat in Belitsky's office (overlooking the Winter Palace), who, I think, was in charge of the administration of the Petrograd Soviet (and who also published Vsevolod Ivanov).

They were talking about issuing mittens to the police.

"I would also like to have a pair," Merezhkovsky said.

Belitsky wrote a note.

Then Merezhkovsky asked:

"Two more: for Zinaida Nikolaevna Gippius and for Filosofov." But people lived without mittens in those days.

In 1915 Khlebnikov published his proposals in the journal *Vzyal* (*Took*). There was a good deal of ironic sense in them. Velimir was proposing to designate numbers to common phrases as it is done with paragraphs or articles of laws. It would have been marvelous.

"Sixty-nine!" They would yell at me from the journal *Na postu*, which would be some kind of insult. "One hundred and twelve!" I would yell back, saving my time.

The numbers would also include quotes.

Sergei Tretyakov is proposing something similar in his play *I Want a Baby*. But only for the sake of swearing.

Velimir also proposed building houses with iron bases and mobile glass boxes. Each person would have the right to own a cubage in such a building in any city.

It was brilliantly conceived.

Apartment-living, sedentariness, fate were taken negatively.

There is nothing more deplorable than fate.

If you ask, especially women, in the village what the neighboring village is called, they often don't know. Fate has bound them to the hut with the mooing of the cow.

We lived before the revolution bound to fate as unhappy Greek sponges bound to the bottom of the sea. You get born, gain strength. Then you accidentally come across a profession and you live like that. And there were many remarkable poets who lived alongside synodic officials and insurance agents.

Such an interesting thing as human fate is arranged awfully in a capitalistic society. And so during the revolution there was no such thing as fate.

There is plenty of time if one isn't worrying about mittens, and the kingdom of freedom is anticipated by the weightless, but the already voluminous.

Go wherever you want, open a school for theater prompters for the Red Fleet, talk on the theory of rhythm in a hospital—there will always be an audience. People were willing to give you their attention. The world had let go of the anchors.

I am thirty-four years old, and I remember most of those years.

And I would like to move the memory of two or three years of my life forward and see anew what we call military communism.

The city was hungry but free even with the curfew and the night patrol in the streets.

We owe our inventions to that time—there was enough wind for all the sails.

Dostoevsky, Jerome K. Jerome (who died recently), and the still restless Merezhkovsky all unanimously declared that socialism is boredom.

I will refute that as a witness.

We ignored the bitterness of life and the necessity to fix it and it seems that we were happy. We just didn't have enough carbohydrates and proteins to fortify this kingdom of intellectual freedom under the guns of "Aurora."

A MOST ABSURD DEATH

It is very hard for me to write this. The past tense is so unsuitable for the deceased. How can you write about a person whose term was cut short? A most absurd death. There was Gorky in a frock coat and crew-cut hair. The sly and omniscient Sukhanov. The very young Mayakovsky. Today you won't find such young people.

And there was Larisa Reisner.

With blond plaits. Northern face. At once both timid and self-assured.

She wrote reviews in *Letopis* and an epic poem of universal significance, of course, as it is done at the age of nineteen, titled "Atlantis," I think.

We were moving into the world then as one might move into a new apartment.

Larisa Mikhailovna loved skating. She liked being seen on the rink. Later on she worked for the amateur student magazines *Rudin*, I think, and *Bohème*.

As a writer, as a northerner, Reisner matured slowly.

Then the revolution came. Like wind in a sail.

Larisa Mikhailovna was among those who took the Peter and Paul Fortress. Not a difficult assault. The difficult part was approaching the fortress. Having the faith that the gates would open.

The first meeting of *Novaya Zhizn* (*New Life*). Reisner was saying something. Steklov, horrified, kept asking people next to him: "Is she a Marxist?" And at that time Larisa Mikhailovna was already involved, I believe, in the reform of Russian orthography.

She was not a thinker yet, she was only twenty-two. She was talented and dared to live. People think they will taste a great deal of life, but they only sample it.

Reisner was greedy for life. And in life she kept spreading her sails as widely as possible.

She was sailing on a half wind course. Her path was cut across.

She described the Winter Palace really well. She could see its comic side.

She was with the Bolsheviks when we thought they were a sect. Blok then used to say bitterly that the majority of humanity belonged to "the Right SR Party."

I remember Larisa Mikhailovna at the Loskutnaya Hotel. She was then Raskolnikov's wife. The fleet was almost on the Moscow River.

It was so crowded that it was almost embarrassing.

I was in the enemy camp. When I changed my mind and returned, Larisa welcomed me as a best comrade would. With her northern, parsonic bearing that was somehow good.

Then she went off with the Volga Flotilla.

She packed her life so eagerly, as if she was packing for good and going to another planet.

Raskolnikov's destroyers crossed the sandbanks and traced a red line along the Volga.

There, in the campaigns, Larisa Reisner found her literary style.

It was not a woman's style of writing. And it was not the habitual irony of a journalist either.

Irony is a cheap way of being clever.

Larisa Mikhailovna held dear what she saw and took life seriously. Perhaps in a heavy-weighted and overloaded way. But then life itself was as overcrowded as a railroad car.

Reisner matured slowly and didn't get old. She didn't train her hand. The best pieces that she wrote were her most recent articles—the brilliant descriptions of Ullstein, the Junkers factories. She understood Germany really well.

A true reporter who didn't have an editorial point of view.

Being mentored by the Acmeists and Symbolists, Larisa Reisner knew how to see things.

In Russian journalism her style departed from the bookish style the most.

That's because she was one of the most cultured.

And that's how extravagantly this journalist was made.

Larisa Mikhailovna had only just begun to write. She did not believe in herself, she kept re-educating herself.

Her best article is on Baron von Steingel ("The Decembrists," I think, is only now being published).

She had just learned not to describe or name the object, but to extend it.

And here is an alien face in the familiar hall at the House of the Press.

How many times have we seen her here!

A live piece has been torn, as if with teeth, from Russian journalism.

Friends will never forget Larisa Reisner.

ZORICH

The title of this article is against the rules of constructing a feuilleton, as indeed I will be writing about Zorich here.

In order to correct my mistake, I will start with Lev Sosnovsky. *Ogonyok* (*Little Flame*) recently published some of his feuilletons in a separate chapbook.

Sosnovsky is a good agronomist, but he also writes articles on music and literature.

Had he not been a feuilletonist, it would have meant that he is working outside of his field of specialization.

But Sosnovsky is working in his field of specialization as a feuilletonist.

Lomonosov once suggested connecting "distant ideas" in the same line in odes, and now they are doing this in the feuilleton.

The concept of the feuilleton is rather broad and has been developing historically and not as a result of analysis. People talk about the "small feuilleton," the "feuilleton-novel." But from the point of view of technique, the main features of the feuilleton should be: 1) its connection to the newspaper and the theme of the day, and 2) its inclusion of several intentionally unrelated ("distant") themes.

The new themes can be introduced from the very beginning with a startling title, after which the reader experiences an abrupt transition as he reads the first line of the feuilleton. This kind of title is usually explained in the final lines of the feuilleton, thus resolving it. Often the feuilleton consists of two or three facts, told in parallel manner, or it begins with a random and strange fact, from where it suddenly jumps to the theme of the day.

Sosnovsky has a feuilleton titled "Let's Not Bow to Foreigners, Let's Bow to Our Mother-Land."

It was written during negotiations regarding a loan agreement with the British government. Its (main) content was an agitation campaign for growing root vegetables.

There is no logic in the juxtaposition of turnips against the loan agreement, as one can grow turnips using the loan money, but the feuilleton's principle is employed correctly here, i.e. the subject should be pitched in a least expected context.

Doroshevich's technique—short, disconnected sentences—became accepted as a feuilleton style because it achieves the same effect of unexpected perception.

Sosnovsky founded the Society for Economic Scouting. Scouting, not Studies.

Every case, perceived in its own system, in its genesis, is always logical. The British Circumlocution Office, about which Dickens wrote, was undeniably the most historical and genetically correctly grown establishment.

But while taking logic into account, the journalist-feuilletonist ignores genesis; he juxtaposes "distant things" and pulls out separate facts with the help of scouting.

From this perspective, feuilletonists, who represent neither an establishment nor a labor union, are indispensable. The feuilletonist can almost always be, if not refuted, then dismissed with phrases such as "an isolated fact" or "the inevitable belch of a rotten way of life."

But nobody can complain against a feuilleton.

Soviet feuilletons differ from their predecessors, the pre-Soviet feuilletons, in their style: they are less broken-up.

In some feuilletons the shift is given on too large a material.

The Soviet feuilletonist uses facts, letters, and protocols more often.

The best of Sosnovsky's feuilletons are based on that principle.

Sometimes the artist selects a single expression from a document and turns it into a title and a flowing image against the background of which the entire piece is experienced anew.

"The Important Thing Is Not to Be Shy" and "The Ukase of the Duke of Richelieu" by Sosnovsky as well as Zorich's "A Cavalry Fool" are of this kind.

One should not think that the orientation toward the material excludes the artist's work. Leskov used to buy old archives and his own works are a mix of selections from this material (Eichenbaum). Tolstoy's story "What For?" is contaminated with quotations from Maksimov (Tynjanov).

The feuilleton underwent a dramatic change in Zorich's work. His main topic is the province. The province is given through a document and a story—a physiological sketch without a plot.

Physiological sketches, as seen in English and Russian (but not German) literature, correspond to the pre-novel period, a period when the old form of the plot is not felt, but the material itself is starting to be perceived aesthetically.

Sketches by Boz for Dickens naturally morphed into *The Pickwick Papers*.

Zorich usually doesn't have plotted constructions, though he knows what plot is, as one can see in his excellent story "About a Kopek."

But plot is often replaced with a juxtaposition of narrative voice against events: "Pre-trial hearings begin ... 'regarding noise in the birch grove.'" The accused Komsomol worker is interrogated based on Articles 99, 162, 168, and 187 of the Criminal Code. This is followed by a serious description of the case. The Komsomol worker defends himself against the accusation by quoting in Latin: "*Audiatur et altera pars.*" The style of the feuilleton "About a Cauliflower" is based on the same principle, but with a difference that the mock ceremoniousness ends with imprisonment.

But the important thing in Zorich's feuilletons is something else: they don't stand in isolation, but are connected to the entire page of the newspaper. Their "feuilletonness," if you will, emerges on the border between Zorich's piece and the neighboring articles. Zorich's feuilletons are feuilletons set against the background of articles about Chamberlain.

Stylistically Zorich is closely associated with Leskov and even more so with Gogol, often repeating their intonations. But as a feuilletonist, he is utterly original.

Though the literary merits of Zorich's works exceed the newspaper level, I think they will lose much of their meaning outside the newspaper.

They will lose more than the feuilletons of Sosnovsky or Koltsov.

Zorich is reprinting his works in a separate chapbook. I would advise him to at least furnish the chapbook with newspaper clippings, epigraphs, and quotations.

Because the best feuilleton is the one that cannot be extracted from the newspaper.

A COLORED SHOWPIECE

ABOUT THE FEUILLETON

This is how one should have written about the feuilleton.

First, one should have enumerated all the writings that have been called a feuilleton and analyzed everything that has been classified under that term. Then, one should have found out whether the term unifies writings that are essentially similar or that are arbitrarily called one and the same thing.

After clarifying the main similarity of the majority of the material and after differentiating it from other literary phenomena by that same token, we would have been able to give the correct, not the dogmatic definition of the feuilleton.

I am not doing that.

Which is why my analysis here is inevitably dotted-lined.

In my articles on Zorich and Sosnovsky in *Zhurnalist* (*The Journalist*) I was suggesting that some writings in contemporary prose are ascribed to the feuilleton genre not due to their inner structure, but due to their place of publication.

It is a most curious case where function defines genre.

Zorich's feuilleton, published outside of the newspaper, is belletristic writing. The specific feature of the old, pre-revolution feuilleton was the diversity and lightness of its themes. The old feuilleton had a distinctly literary way of showing unusual associations.

THE REVOLUTION BROUGHT CHANGES TO THE FEUILLETON GENRE

It expanded.

The themes in the feuilleton were reduced.

We talk about the lightness of the feuilleton only in the past tense.

Now the feuilleton consists of only two or three themes.

One theme is targeted—it is programmatic. The feuilleton is not named after the targeted theme but after the supplementary, estranging theme. The supplementary theme is introduced to change the key in which the targeted theme is usually perceived.

The art of the feuilletonist is thus the unexpected and definite (not overstretched) decoding of the main theme with the help of the estranging theme.

Sometimes the estranging theme has an unhappy ending, as in novellas.

That is (it's nice to start a sentence with *that is*), the theme that changes the main one is external to the feuilleton.

So, for example, Sosnovsky described the behavior of some hooligan with a tone that justified his actions.

The feuilletonness of the device lies in the estrangement of the theme through narration, through the introduction of an unmentioned narrator as it were.

Perhaps it is tone that explains the ascribing of works such as "Chamberlain's Dream" and other "fantastic" articles to the genre of the feuilleton.

The estrangement of the factual material in these articles is feuilletonic.

But reduced to a single theme, they are on the margin of the genre.

THE CLASSICAL SOVIET FEUILLETON

It is represented by Mikhail Koltsov.

He always has two or three themes in his feuilletons.

Koltsov's achievement is that he knows how to take into account the timbre of his themes and to never bring themes of the same type into the same feuilleton.

It is interesting that even in his articles, for example, the one in which he is describing a flight over the Black Sea, Koltsov makes use of the feuilletonic device of introducing a second theme based on a distant associative link. More than anything, this follows the logic of the old feuilleton.

BROADENING OF THE GENRE

In provincial and professional newspapers, the feuilleton now is a staged article with a single theme that has belletristic features.

There is also a type of feuilleton with an epigraph—a theme, which later is feuilletonized.

Sosnovsky's declaration during one of the debates implies that same tendency to broaden the concept of the genre: "Open the last page of *Gudok* (*The Whistle*) and you will find at least twenty to thirty feuilletonists there."

The implication, of course, is misleading, as you will find on that page the work of five or six correctors who stage worker-correspondent[34] material in dialogues.

But Sosnovsky is more determined than you think. He calls Richter's sketches feuilletons and proposes "to feuilletonize our newspaper from an advanced to a murderous chronicle" (*Zhurnalist*, January 1926).

Here the genre dies from an enlarged heart.

Sosnovsky's device is feuilletonic.

Only a feuilletonist can propose to write feuilletons out of an announcement.

The word "feuilletonness" is not a term here, but a means to describe the feuilleton—to unexpectedly flip the concept.

Of course, one could ask: Why work on the term? Why clarify what a feuilleton is? Moliere's explanation should suffice, after all: "Opium makes one drowsy because it has a sleep-inducing power."

The feuilleton is what has been over-feuilletonized. But you can't cure anything with that.

It is impossible to have a newspaper comprised of only feuilletons.

You can't tell the difference without comparison.

---

34   In 1918, the newspaper *Pravda* initiated a movement to recruit worker correspondents (*rabkor*) and peasant correspondents (*selkor*) from the newly literate strata of society to act as informants or co-authors, who would provide the common citizen's perspective.

THE MECHANISM OF THE FEUILLETON RESISTS
THE CROSS-POLLINATION OF THE GENRE

Sometimes only the title in a feuilleton remains as a feuilleton, but then it is also a theme.

Recently Koltsov, a pureblood feuilletonist, wrote an article about newspaper clichés, about "standing ovations," "overfilled halls," and so on.

It is clearly a feuilleton. You can tell from its title: "The Drowning Coffin."

This is only but one of the clichés, estranged by the mere truncation of the last part of the expression "the coffin was drowning in flowers."

But the coffin can also be a *theme*. The coffin, as an image in the vernacular, means boredom, failure. A "sinking coffin" is a theme of a rather sinister shipwreck.

Zorich did something similar once by titling an article about oratorical clichés (in their village refractions)—"A Con Joker."

It means, simply, conjuncture. The phrase "con joker" is just an example of folk etymology. The title is a quote from the article.

But this title, like the one that I referred to earlier, has its own refraction. We get a theme about some stupid, insolent charlatan.

Zorich's stories too, the ones that get published in newspapers, are feuilletons. This appears to us as the most interesting "debate on coloring."

Here the argument is not about the line between article and feuilleton, but between feuilleton and "story."

Zorich received letters from his readers. They didn't propose material in those letters. Instead, the material in those letters protested. A border guard once wrote about Zorich's feuilleton "An Incident from Orlovshchina."

The feuilleton is about a man who runs over an old woman who happens to be a teacher.

The feuilleton gives all the details, including the conversations.

It is with regard to these details that the border guard protested in his letter: How could Zorich possibly know that the secretary (the man who had run over the old woman) yelled to the carriage driver "Go! Drive!" and not "Please go!" or "Fast!" or something else?

How could the feuilletonist know, sitting in his Moscow office, how dry or polite the secretary was with the old teacher and how his facial expression changed when he found out her social position?

The border guard thinks that the invented part weakens or even destroys the social significance of the feuilleton because it engenders suspicion and mistrust in the reader toward fact itself, which lies at the basis of writing.

It is an interesting letter.

Zorich responded by saying that he is "for coloring."

"Because it is not enough to just give the negative fact, you must tell about it so that the story captures the reader alive."

I AM AGAINST COLORING

I don't know about the reader, but if I were the fact itself, I would have preferred being handled in a different way.

If I read that a sportsman ran a certain distance in 2.05 minutes, instead of 2.1 minutes, the difference of 0.05 minutes interests me as a fact.

But I am less interested when I read in a story that a hero without an address ran the whole distance in 2 minutes.

Imagine that you are reading a story about the revolutionary Kamo, for example. He committed some incredible, almost impossible deeds.

You could add, invent even more incredible things. But there is no need for that. We devalue the accomplishment with such embellishments.

We must not add or invent out of respect for the accomplishment.

Invention devalues the 0.05 minutes.

And the newspaper day consists of real fractions.

Zorich is a talented feuilletonist, but he placed dummies amid living human beings. He wouldn't have done so if he had a better sense of the genre.

THE IMPORTANCE OF THE FEUILLETON TODAY

The feuilleton and its success today, which we still haven't been able to properly assess, is due to its form, which allows one to work with real facts.

The joyful sensation—the sensation of the shift, the turn of the material—is given between and not within the pieces.

Coloring the patterns in embroidery was generally considered to be in bad taste.

The embroiderer was not supposed to circumvent the difficulties.

One had to work seriously on the cross-stitch patterns.

These are the times of literary reaction.

To praise a writer is to say that he is working not worse than so and so. And the ten years between "so and so" and what they are writing today is considered to be a loss.

The feuilleton contains the elements of a different approach.

It is part of a new genre.

Writing off the feuilleton into the category of fiction means to write oneself off as a loss.

ISAAC BABEL

A CRITICAL ROMANCE[35]

I somehow feel bad for examining Babel so closely. One should respect a writer's success and give the reader time to like an author without yet finding out about his success. I am ashamed for examining Babel too closely. He has the following passage in "The Rabbi's Son": "The girls, their bandy bovine legs firmly planted on the floor, stared coolly at his sexual organs, the withered, curly manhood of the emaciated Semite."[36]

And I have to rev up the lyrical engine for this article on Babel.

Once there was old Russia, huge, like an expansive mountain with furrowed slopes.

There were people who penciled on it: "This mountain will be saved."

The revolution had not happened yet.

Some of those people who had written in pencil worked at *Letopis*. Gorky, who had just arrived, walked stooped,

35 Footnote by V. Shklovsky—Babel has changed now, but this is the best article that I can write about him.
36 *The Complete Works of Isaac Babel*, ed. Nathalie Babel, trans. Peter Constantine (New York: W. W. Norton, 2002). All subsequent quotations from Babel's stories are taken from this translation.

discontented, sick, and he was writing the article "Two Souls." A completely wrong article. There was a young woman there, Larisa Reisner (before she seized the Peter and Paul Fortress). We were also there, Brik (from 7 Zhukovskaya Street) and I in my leather pants and jacket from the armored car unit. The journal was full of loose and layered belletristic writings that weren't even remotely close to old hay. The difference between those who wrote in the journal was only in their surnames.

But Bazarov also wrote for *Letopis*, Sukhanov stung like a horsefly, and Mayakovsky got published there too.

One of the issues included a story by Babel.

It was about two girls who tried unsuccessfully to do an abortion. Their father was the prosecutor in Kamchatka. Everyone noticed that story and remembered it. That's when I met Babel. Average height, high forehead, big head, face that doesn't belong to a writer, dark clothes, a great conversant.

Then the revolution came, and the mountain was cleared away. Some people ran after it with their pencil. They had nothing to write on.

That's when Sukhanov started to write. Seven tomes of memoirs. They say he wrote them before the events took place, since he foresaw everything.

I arrived from the front. It was autumn. *Novaya zhizn* was still in print.

Babel wrote for a section there called "A New Way of Life." He was the only one who preserved his stylistic composure during the revolution. The section published articles about new tilling methods. It was then that I became better acquainted with him. He seemed to be a person with an engaged voice that was never anxious and was full of pathos.

He needed pathos as much as he needed a country house.

I met Babel for the third time in Petersburg in 1919. In the winter, Petersburg was covered in snow. It stood against snowdrifts as a latticed railroad shield. In the summer, a clear blue sky covered the city. There was no smoke coming from the chimneys, and the unhindered sun stood above the horizon. Petersburg was empty—everyone had gone to the front. The green grass crept up from under the cobblestones and burst like flames toward the sun.

The backstreets were already overgrown.

They played *gorodki* in front of the Hermitage, on the busted wood block pavements. The city was overgrowing like an abandoned military camp.

Babel lived on 25 October Prospect, in the house #86. He lived alone in the fully furnished rooms; others came and went. He had maidservants who looked after him, cleaned the rooms, took out buckets with floating——.

Babel lived his life, observing unhurriedly the hungry lechery of the city. His own room was clean. He would tell me that nowadays women could be had mostly before six, because the trams stopped running after that.

He was not alienated from life. But it did seem to me that Babel, before going to bed, would sign each and every lived day—as if it were a story. The instruments of the man's trade had left their trace on him.

Babel always had a samovar and often bread on his table, which was a rarity in those days.

He was always a warm and welcoming host. One of his frequent visitors was a former chemist, a Tolstoyan, who told incredible anecdotes. He had insulted the Grand Duke of Baden and came to the trial from Switzerland in order to testify against himself (but he was declared insane and they only confiscated his laboratory). He was also a bad poet and a mediocre reviewer.

The name of this most incredible man was Pyotr Storitsyn. Babel was very fond of him. There were also others who frequented his place including Kondrat Yakovlev, a few others, myself, some handicapped men, and others from Odessa who were ready-made stories and who told things straight out of books. Babel wrote little, but he wrote persistently. It was always the same story—about two Chinese men in a brothel.

He loved that story as he loved Storitsyn. The Chinese men and the women kept changing. They grew young, aged, broke glasses, beat up women, arranged for this and that. A good many stories resulted from all this. One sunny autumn day, without resolving the question of his Chinese men, Babel left, leaving me his gray sweater and leather suitcase. Yuri Annenkov later borrowed the suitcase from me without ever returning. We didn't hear from Babel; it was as though he had gone to Kamchatka to tell the prosecutor about his daughters.

Once a visiting Odessite, who had been losing at cards all night in a mutual friend's house, and who in the morning borrowed money to cover his losses, told as a sign of gratitude that Babel was either translating from French or putting together a book of stories from a book of anecdotes.

Later, when I was wounded and passing through Kharkov, I heard that Babel had been killed in the Red Cavalry.

Fate unhurriedly took us through a hundred reversals.

I met Babel again in 1924. I learned from him that he had not been killed, though they beat him for a long time.

He hadn't changed much. His narrative had become even more interesting.

He brought two books with him—one from Odessa and the other from the front. The Chinese men had been forgotten, they had found their own way into one of the stories.

The new works were masterfully written. I doubt that we have anyone who writes better today.

Readers compare him to Maupassant because they sense a French influence and hasten to cite a praiseworthy name.

I suggest another name—Flaubert. And especially the Flaubert of *Salammbô*.

One of the finest librettos ever written for opera.

The shiniest riding boots resembling young women, the whitest breeches, as white as a banner splitting the sky, even a fire blazing as bright as Sunday, cannot be compared to Babel's style.[37]

A foreigner from Paris, from Paris alone, *sans* London, Babel saw Russia the way that a French writer attached to Napoleon's army might have seen it.

He no longer needed the Chinese men, they were replaced by Cossacks from French illustrations.

Experts in flattery say that it's best to praise with abusive words.

"The significance and force of using a word, the lexical coloring of which is juxtaposed against its intonational coloring, lies in the very sensation of this non-coincidence."[38]

The significance of Babel's device is in his manner of speaking about stars and gonorrhea in one voice.

Babel does not succeed in the lyrical parts.

His descriptions of Brody, the abandoned Jewish cemetery, are not so great.

Babel adopts an elevated tone in his descriptions and lists many beautiful things. He writes in "Line and Color":

37 References to Babel's stories "My First Goose" and "Prishchepa."
38 Yuri Tynjanov, "The Problem of Verse Language," 1924.

You and I are walking through this enchanted garden, this marvelous Finnish forest. To our dying day we will not encounter anything better, and you, you cannot even see the rosy, ice-crusted edges of the waterfall, over there, on the river. The weeping willow, leaning over the waterfall—you cannot see its Japanese delicacy. The red trunks of the pine trees heaped with snow! The granular sparkle that scintillates over the snows! It begins as a frozen line above the tree's wavy surface, like Leonardo's line, crowned by the reflection of the blazing clouds. And what about Fröken Kristi's silk stockings, and the line of her maturing legs?

It is true, though, that this passage ends with the following line: "I beg of you, Alexander Fyodorovich, buy some spectacles!"

The clever writer knows how to vindicate the beauty of his works through irony at the right moment.

It would be shameful to read such things without the irony. And he anticipates our objection by placing a heading over his pictures—"opera":

The burned-out town—broken columns and the hooks of evil old women's fingers dug into the earth—seemed to me raised into the air, comfortable and unreal like a dream. The naked shine of the moon poured over the town with unquenchable strength. The damp mold of the ruins blossomed like a marble bench on the opera stage. And I waited with anxious soul for Romeo to descend from the clouds, a satin Romeo singing of love, while backstage a dejected electrician waits with his finger on the button to turn off the moon.[39]

39 From "Italian Sun."

I have compared *Red Cavalry* with *Taras Bulba*: there are similarities in certain devices. The story "A Letter" reworks Gogol's plot by having one of the sons kill their father. Babel also adopts Gogol's device of enumerating surnames, which perhaps is coming from the classical tradition. But the enumeration in Babel is interrupted. This is how Savitsky, the Cossack commander, writes in "The Continuation of the Story of a Horse":

> Thirty days I have been fighting in the rear guard, covering the retreat of the invincible First Red Cavalry, and finding myself facing powerful gunfire from airplanes and artillery. Tardy was killed, Lukhmannikov was killed, Lykoshenko was killed, Gulevoy was killed, Trunov was killed, and the white stallion is no longer under me, so with the change in our fortunes of war, Comrade Khlebnikov, do not expect to see your beloved Division Commander Savitsky ever again. To tell you the truth, we shall meet again in the Kingdom of Heaven, although, from what people say, the old man up there in heaven isn't running a kingdom, but an all-out whorehouse, and as it is we have enough clap down here on earth—so, who knows, we might not get to see each other after all. Farewell, Comrade Khlebnikov.

The Cossacks in Babel are all insufferably and indescribably handsome. "Indescribably" is Babel's favorite word. But his allusions create different backgrounds.

Babel uses two contradictions that replace the function of plot: 1) style vs. way of life, and 2) way of life vs. author.

He is a stranger in the army, a foreigner with the right to be surprised. He underscores the "weakness and despair" of the observer when describing the military way of life.

Besides *Red Cavalry*, Babel has *The Odessa Stories*. They are full of descriptions about bandits. Babel needs the bandits' pathos and speckled junk to justify his style.

If the commander of the division was wearing "riding boots resembling young women" ("My First Goose") then "the Moldavanka aristocrats were jammed into crimson vests, their shoulders encased in chestnut-colored jackets, and their fleshy legs bulged in sky-blue leather boots" ("The King").

Babel is a foreigner in both countries. He is a foreigner in Odessa too. They tell him there: "Well then, forget for a while that you have glasses on your nose and autumn in your heart. Forget that you pick fights from behind your desk and stutter when you are out in the world! Imagine for a moment that you pick fights in town squares and stutter only among papers" ("How Things Were Done in Odessa").

Of course, this is not Babel's portrait.

Babel is not like that at all: he doesn't stutter. He is brave, and I even think that he "can spend the night with a Russian woman, and the Russian woman will be satisfied" with him ("How Things Were Done in Odessa").

Because the Russian woman loves eloquence. Babel pretends to be a foreigner because this device, just as irony, eases the writing. Even Babel doesn't risk writing pathos without irony.

Babel mutes the music when describing a dance in his writing and at the same time renders the whole piece in a high register. And he probably borrows the device of answers that repeat the question from the epic poem.

He applies this device everywhere.

Benya Krik says in "How Things Were Done in Odessa":

Grach asked him, "Who're you, where d'you come from, what's your bread and butter?"

"Try me, Froim," Benya answered, "and let's stop wasting time spreading kasha on the table."

"Fine, we won't waste time spreading kasha on the table," Grach said. "I'll try you."

And the Cossacks in "A Letter" speak in the same way:

And Semyon asked our Papa, Timofey Rodyonich, "So, Papa, are you feeling good now that you're in my hands?"

"No," Papa said, "I'm feeling bad."

Then Semyon asked him, "And my brother Fyodor, when you were hacking him to pieces, did he feel good in your hands?"

"No," Papa said, "Fyodor was feeling bad."

Then Semyon asked him, "And did you think, Papa, that someday you might be feeling bad?"

"No," Papa said, "I didn't think that I might be feeling bad."

Babel's books—are good books.

Russian literature is as gray as a siskin, it needs purple breeches and sky-blue leather boots.

It also needs what Babel understood when he left his Chinese men to fend for themselves and plunged into *Red Cavalry*.

Literary heroes, girls, old men, young people and their situations have already been exhausted. Literature needs concreteness and hybridization with the new social reality for the creation of a new form.

CONTEMPORARIES AND SYNCHRONISTS

The story behind this piece is the following:
I read my name in *Russky Sovremennik* (*The Russian
Contemporary*) next to the names of Abram Efros,
Kozma Prutkov and some other classic.
Then I wrote a letter to *Russky Sovremennik*.
In the letter I expressed my surprise at the fact that
I was appearing as the contemporary of Tyutchev
and Putkov without refuting the fact itself, but
categorically refuting my contemporaneity with Efros
and Khodasevich and asserting that it was only a
chronological illusion. The letter was not published,
and this article is just using the theme.

I met the late Lev Lunts years ago when he was still a boy. His
every other word was "my meme."

His "meme" and his father had gone abroad. Lunts opted
to stay.

Lunts was from a middle-class bourgeois family. It gave him
at least a good background in foreign languages. Just like any
boy, Lunts liked to read Dumas, Stevenson, Captain Marryat.
Every boy under "meme's" influence, the influence of tradition,
abandons children's literature and moves on to Turgenev and
Veresaev. Lunts opted to stay.

Being a very educated person for his age and a well-read philologist, he was nonetheless stuck in his youthful romanticism and adventure fiction. His traditional parents (nice people) were gone, and Lunts was writing a funny epistolary novel about respectable people traveling across the border and carrying money in a garment brush. The brush was stolen, which led to a mad rush to buy up every brush on the border. The novel ends with a shopkeeper's letter ordering "two more boxcars of garment brushes of the same kind."

Lev Lunts was like grass that had grown in a cleared forest.

Fate had freed him from compromises.

His works remain unpublished because they are not traditional. Our contemporaries like most of all young writers who write not worse than the old writers, and that is the great fault of the friends of Leonov who is not a bad writer.

Lunts's friends are losing their youthfulness now.

Mikhail Slonimsky, who started with first-rate sketches and Soviet folk tales, is now writing conventional stories. *The Emery Machine* is a capable book, but it wasn't worth writing.

One shouldn't strive to carry out the assignments of old theaters. One shouldn't get carried away with theme. One shouldn't say "my meme."

Mother is gone.

We ought to stop "preserving the culture," hand the museums over to the State Treasury, with the right to review, and study methods in old literature instead of themes. Theme is taking up too much space now. It seems sufficient to proletarian writers for the creation of new literature, and yet it oppresses Akhmatova.

Theme has driven Yesenin into the pubs and won't let him out; he must drink and sway as a drunk.

Kazin is writing about all of his relatives, one by one.

And even Mayakovsky is imprisoned by his theme: revolution and love that keeps apologizing for coming during the revolution.

And what is theme in poetry?

A nail on which one can hang himself, or just hang his hat.

Poets are already running from the spheres taken up by their themes. Where is Mayakovsky now?

"Nowhere but in Mosselprom," or "Can be found—in Gosizdat."[40]

Let him loaf around all he wants, theme doesn't bother him there—he will have enough of it soon.

I have written a very long introduction. But there isn't going to be an article anyway, and introductions get in the way of only young writers.

Writers appear in literature variously: with or without introductions.

Writers appearing in literature with introductions, as a general rule, do not have a long life.

I remember how they started talking about Yesenin: it had a theatrical effect, at first you hear the buzz, then specific sounds, and suddenly the name is born.

As a rather old journalist, let me expound here the rules for removing a writer from literature.

This is how it's done these days. They begin by chiding the person in the spotlight. They usually do it by shouting that he is "talented, but harmful"—typically only the first half of the phrase is remembered. They didn't devour people like that before.

40   Advertising slogans for Mosselprom (Moscow Agricultural Industries) and Gosizdat (State Publishing House) written by Mayakovsky.

People were chided in subordinate clauses, as if in passing. Those wishing to familiarize themselves with this technique can read Tolstoy's account in *Anna Karenina*—that's how they devour Levin's brother. One ought to chide without paying attention.

I want everyone to know this, because I like high technique in everything.

But let us return to Yesenin, who is probably starting to worry.

I saw Yesenin for the first time in the salon of Zinaida Gippius. He was already in disfavor.

"What are those strange gaiters you are wearing?" Zinaida Gippius asked, examining Yesenin's feet through her lorgnette.

"These are felt boots," he replied.

Gippius, of course, knew that felt boots were not gaiters and Yesenin too knew why he was being asked that question. Gippius's question meant: I can't seem to recall . . . I don't believe in your felt boots, you are no peasant.

And Yesenin's response: Leave me alone, I don't need you.

This is how it was done back then.

Meanwhile, the whole argument was about the October Revolution.

But I knew Yesenin from before. He was young, handsome, with golden locks, blue eyes, spoke marvelously. Yesenin's trouble was that he wore those felt boots in the city for too long. Art didn't appear to him as an outgrowth of culture, as a sum of knowledge—of competence (according to Trotsky) with an expanded experience. Yesenin's poetic theme is "the lost, fallen Yesenin." It may be as heavy for him as wearing felt boots in summer time, but he doesn't write poems, he merely extends his own theme poetically.

Yesenin's mistake is that he doesn't know how to differentiate the days of the month from patronal feast days. This is perhaps a peasant's mistake.

The day of the month—is competence; a feast day—is a theme connected to a day.

And the peasantry lives only from feast day to feast day.

I remember how Nikolai Tikhonov emerged as a writer. At first, a rumor spread in the studios in Leningrad that a Red Cavalryman, an Unteroffizier, is writing poetry, in fact, bad poetry but with exquisite lines. Then Tikhonov himself appeared. He was thin, dressed smartly, soldier-like. He settled in the lower level of the House of Arts, in the long, dark, and cold corridor with Vsevolod Rozhdestvensky. There was an iron stove in the middle of the room, the firewood was under the beds. Tikhonov and Rozhdestvensky shared the table by the window for writing. Once the House of Arts organized an evening event. Kusikov danced lezginka on the table to the great indignation of the dishes and Tikhonov read his "Makhno." Later some fifteen young people slept in his room on the floor, and in the morning he offered them tea from a single pot.

Dear young contemporaries, beware of karakul sheep farming—the hasty birth of poets and prose writers! The skin is beautiful, but the lamb is premature. The bitter cold in the corridor of the House of Arts, the military service and breaking ice on the street did not harm Tikhonov. The fact that no journals were published in Russia for two or three years was also healthy for the young writers. They wrote for themselves.

Tikhonov does not cling to his felt boots. He grows, changes, reads the history of naval warfare and studies English. He knows the difference between the date of the month and a feast day. He knows that St. George's Day—the day when the cows are sent out for grazing—has nothing to do with St. George's merits. Having a commendable biography and a real man's posture, he does not merely write about himself, but breaks through Russian culture: he has learned from Gumilyov, Kipling, Pasternak, and now he is learning from Khlebnikov. And this work preserves Tikhonov's idealism. He hasn't changed at all: he is wearing the same scarf around his neck and his gaunt cheeks are the same, as though they had been sliced with a knife.

And now, I can finally talk about Vsevolod Ivanov. We used to take off our coats together with the sacks—without removing the sleeves from the straps. We said then that the sack would become part of every Russian's outfit, as the collar used to be.

Once Gorky said to me in a low voice: "There is a young writer, a typesetter—do you want to meet him?" I told him that I did. Gorky described him and gave me some money for him.

I caught Vsevolod Ivanov on the Fontanka, right across from the Chinizelli Circus and took him to the only bookstore in Petersburg called "The Book Corner." We saw Khovin sitting in a corner, drinking tea from a yellow kettle and pretending to be a bookseller. There were only five buyers in Petersburg, and they were all booksellers.

Vsevolod was very thin back then, with a face that someone would have after typhus, red faded hair, and a beard that had the color and dignity of horsehair worms. He wore a sheepskin jacket without a collar, buttons and fur inside. He wrapped his feet in cloth and wore self-made shoes that were tightly tied with wire. He looked at me wildly and mistrustfully, but he took the money.

A week later Vsevolod was reading a story at a Serapion Brotherhood gathering but he stood mostly by the wall, which was later explained by the condition of his trousers. Ivanov had already arrived in Petersburg with many pieces of writing, his peculiar manner, and he wrote in Petersburg the whole time—with great ease and in an interesting way.

We were under the impression that he was exceptionally talented, that he was profuse in imagery because it cost him nothing. He wasn't afraid of making mistakes because he didn't know most of the rules. His first works were colorful, themes about rural life, Asiatic peasantry. Ivanov and Nikitin established the Eastern wing of the Serapion Brotherhood. But apart from "The Kid," which was meticulously censored and banned for a long time, Ivanov had another line, which had not been noticed at first by almost anyone. In "The Kid," Vsevolod demonstrated his knowledge of how to build a plot and understand the irony of artistic construction. Primitive mastery and trade in ethnography didn't really interest him. Vsevolod was immediately labeled according to his theme: a writer of the peasantry, elemental painter, Asiatic. But he didn't insist on the felt boots.

The three years in literature prior to this for Ivanov were perhaps only three cups of foam poured into the ground, so that the fourth could be filled with wine. Now Vsevolod is swiftly moving toward the West—toward plot, toward H. G. Wells, and this movement is not accidental, it had been developing from the very first works.

I think that many people remember the content of "The Kid."[41] Partisans from under the Irtysh River are driven by the Whites into Mongolia. Mongolia is a wild and joyless beast, even the butterflies sting there. It is hard for the partisans to get along without women, so they go hunting after Kirgiz women. They lead a dark, stifling existence. One day they come across a suckling child of a killed officer. The child needs care and he won't eat cabbage soup. The partisans go to the Kirgiz camp to seize a cow but luckily also find a Kirgiz woman who has milk. Somehow the woman fetches her own child along and feeds both children—one yellow, the other white—under the watchful eyes of the partisans. This is moving for the reader as he finds himself in familiar realms. Indeed, it is a well-known plot used in Bret Harte's short story "The Luck of Roaring Camp" and in

41 Vsevolod Ivanov, "The Kid," trans. Louis Lozowick (*Broom* 4(3): 1923).

Gorky's or Andreev's story about the birth of a man in a house of thieves and a prostitute. It even reminds one of Chaplin's *The Kid*. The reader is moved by the depiction of these ruthless men who become soft around the kid.

But Ivanov goes on with his story. The partisans love their Vaska and they think that the Kirgiz woman is not feeding the babies equally. They weigh them and indeed Vaska is thinner. "Afanasi Petrovich wrapped the Kirgiz baby in an old sack. The mother whined. Afanasi Petrovich slapped her lightly on the cheek and went into the steppe."

The Kirgiz woman continues to feed the other, white boy under the tender and jovial gaze of the men.

"The peasants looked on, laughing uproariously. Afanasi Petrovich watched them tenderly, blew his nose, and said in a drawl: 'Just watch him go to it.' And behind the canvas tent, the ravine, the steppe, strange Mongolia stretching into unknown distances. Mongolia, wild and joyless beast."

The plot here unfolds in a rather unexpected way. There could be several explanations for this.

We could say that it depicts the extreme ruthlessness of the partisans in the Far East.

But all plots about "converted outlaws" and outlaws who take care of children always imply that these outlaws are cruel. Bret Harte's adventurers probably treated the Native Americans in the same way as the partisans treated the Kirgiz men, women and children.

Those who live in the urban slums are equally cruel to children. Therefore, the material from everyday life that Ivanov uses for his constructions could not have determined a new denouement. The writer chooses from life whatever he needs. The task that Ivanov had set before himself in "The Kid" was probably not to describe the way of life, but to construct a folkloric plot.

Lelevich criticized Ivanov for copying Hoffman in "The Debt." A completely uninformed accusation. It isn't like Hoffmann at all. But from old times Muscovites have always called foreigners Germans.

Being accustomed to the form of the story, cultivated by the literary supplement of Niva, one can certainly confuse Vsevolod Ivanov with Hoffmann. Indeed, "The Debt" is an intricately written story.

The clichéd narrative about the revolution follows this basic line: a Red Army commander is taken prisoner by the Whites, but luckily escapes, pronouncing revolutionary phrases on his way. Sometimes the clichéd ending changes: the commander gets killed. There are hundreds of such stories on the surface of the earth, and many more layers beneath it, lying in baskets under editorial desks.

Ivanov took this plot and put a completely unexpected spin on it. The commander is captured and taken to a green general who … takes him for an acquaintance, an officer to whom he lost in a game of cards, and wants to return his debt.

But this is a false denouement. The general tortures Fadeitsev, compelling him to identify himself and to take back his "debt." Then the Red Army attacks and occupies the village. At this point Fadeitsev finally recalls the circumstances of their first meeting:

Two years ago Fadeitsev was the assistant commandant of the provincial Cheka. He was ordered to escort a convoy of White officers sentenced to death by firing squad. After the execution, Fadeitsev was supposed to check the pulse of the prisoners (for some reason he didn't summon the doctor). Four were killed, the fifth—the tall one, biting his lip, stared at him through his clouded, sand-colored pupils. Fadeitsev was instructed to shoot anyone left alive.

Without lowering his gaze, Fadeitsev took out his revolver, pressed it against the prisoner's chest and pulled the trigger. A misfire. He opened the cylinder—it was empty. He had forgotten to load it again. Now that Fadeitsev had gotten used to death, he could have asked the soldiers to shoot the prisoner, but then he would have to account for his oversight, and he said: "He's dead ... Throw him in ..."

And this was the "debt" between Fadeitsev and the general but they both couldn't recall the incident. Fadeitsev was captured because his revolver wasn't loaded as usual and toward the end of the story Ivanov reestablishes the motive of the revolver to eliminate the possibility of a sentimental ending.

Fadeitsev felt his revolver and moved away from the window.
"Fool ..." he gasped, "Fool ... What a fool!
"Who?"
"Who? What do I know? ... I'd better get some rest, Comrade Karnaukhov!"
And he checked his revolver one more time before going to sleep: it was fully loaded, like an ear of grain at harvest time.[42]

The form of the plot in this work is brilliantly motivated.
Lev Lunts turned out to be right.
The West wins in Russian literature. The Ornamentalists leave their posts and go to re-learn how to write ...
The greatest danger that threatens the writer today is anachronistic competence. There is nothing to be competent in today.

42   Vsevolod Ivanov, "Dolg" [The Debt], 1923.

We really miss Lunts now with his mistakes, desperation, solid knowledge of the old form's death and inexhaustible gaiety of someone who perceives life every day.

Kaverin seems to have taken the route parallel to Lunts's.

But Kaverin learned too easily. He understands the problem schematically, but he has nothing with which to stop the plot scheme. Kaverin is of the Erenburg type, but has not yet fully opened up to "philosophy" or irony. Today Russian prose is splitting into its component parts, as poetry was not too long ago poetry in the hands of the first Futurists: *zaum*, images, etc. Plotted works are being filled with neutral material now—and the material that used to go into plotted works is published elsewhere as diaries or notes.

PRIMARY EDUCATION

ADRIAN PIOTROVSKY—*THE FALL OF YELENA LEI*

I remember in 1919 I was serving as a member of the Repertoire Committee in the Theater Department (later the Petersburg Theater Department). The Arctic Circle was passing then through the Nevsky Prospect and the city seemed dead like a frozen fish. The other committee members were Mikhail Kuzmin, Anna Radlova, Aleksei Remizov, and Adrian Piotrovsky.

The plays kept pouring in endlessly. It seemed strange that the people who wrote and rewrote these thick notebooks didn't know one another and weren't collaborating in some conspiratorial apartment.[43] There were only three or four—no, not even four—types of plays and the most widespread type was the play with presidents and princes. The best work from this herd was Lunts's—"Outside the Law," the rest were Lyuls[44] that only the authors could differentiate.

These plays kept accumulating in layers. Then apparently the layers melted away and we had to listen to everything that was written then.

---

43   A reference to S. An-sky's play "In a Conspiratorial Apartment" (1906).
44   A reference to Aleksei Faiko's play "Lake Lyul," staged by Meyerhold in 1923.

In order not to mix up the newborns in birth clinics, their heels are marked with numbers using ink pens. The task is made easier by the fact that the newborns are either boys or girls, i.e. there is a natural method of classification.

In theater, however, plays with presidents and princes can be classified only alphabetically.

Because of my old friendship with Adrian Piotrovsky I am violating the alphabetical order now.

But here is one more recollection.

In 1921 playwrights were paid per act. There is no doubt that being determines consciousness. The acts kept getting smaller and smaller. We used to write a play per night. I wrote a play that was not bad at all—called *The Cannon of the Commune*—eventually it was lost. All in all, I wrote sixteen plays. The list, I suppose, is in the Playwrights' Union. If someone finds the manuscripts, I am happy to buy them back.

Serious repertory people sit around and argue about Yelenas and Lyuls, thus advertising them … O naïve citizens, the only difficult thing in art is to create something new. You can concoct (without a sacred thrill) as many Yelenas and Lyuls as you please!

These works are counterrevolutionary (or not counterrevolutionary)—you say. These works don't even exist, they haven't been written.

They are only acts and princes.

Adrian Piotrovsky is a talented person. He is knowledgeable and has a unique (not in literature though) physiognomy and his president is not worse than the others.

Moreover, Piotrovsky knows Greek and understands theater. It is probably better to watch his plays than to read them. He knows theater technique. For example, he knows that it is terrifying when someone is beating an iron sheet (which could mean catastrophe) and shouting at the same time, while the lights are off on the stage.

That is how his *Yelena Lei* ends.

In terms of schools, Piotrovsky belongs to Radlov's group.

Radlov wrote similar plays for the theater and used the same kind of eloquence. In its plot, *Yelena Lei* is linked to Aristophanes (*Lysistrata*). But the gender strike is presented as a terrifying strike. Piotrovsky himself is indicating this in the text: "The merchant suddenly spoke in Greek."

Some of the puns are terrible in their unscrupulousness. For example, the play with the word "*vysech*" (meaning both to whip with a switch and to carve out of marble) is already old.

But, of course, Piotrovsky shouldn't get upset over such trifles. *Yelena Lei* is not dangerous if he treats it as a parody.

DOT THE I

ANTOINE ALBALAT'S *THE ART OF WRITING*—A LITERARY PRIMER (WITH A PREFACE BY ARKADI GORNFELD)

There once were thick journals. They lived for about a hundred years. Special people wrote in them—they were not litterateurs or writers but rather journalists. They despised literature.

Have you ever leafed through *Vestnik Yevropy* (*Herald of Europe*)? The journal was in print for a hundred years and always managed to get everything wrong. It was a special drainage canal for removing overconfident talentless hacks. They had their own gods, their own poets and prose writers.

There was another canal, a shorter one, called *Russkoe bogatstvo* (*Russian Wealth*). It descended from glorious parents; its ancestors led literary wars. But the journal itself was left under the care of P.Y.[45]

This is where the writer Vladimir Korolenko *unlearned* how to write, while Nikolai Oliger wrote. And this is where they berated and abused at first the Symbolists (and some others before them) and then the Futurists …

---

45   Probably the poet Pyotr Yakubovich who was one of the editors from 1903-05.

Subjectively speaking, *Russkoe bogatstvo* was an honest journal, but objectively speaking it was a place of literary opposition where the people who wrote badly were against those who wrote well.

Gornfeld was a well-respected man, decorated with many errors. This is how Admiral Makarov was celebrated for his failed attempt to complete an Arctic expedition on the first icebreaker.

Gornfeld wasn't going anywhere and it seems he was very proud of this fact.

He never gave birth to any progeny, literarily speaking, and this is evidently a very aristocratic thing to do. Of course, Gornfeld was smarter than the journal in which he wrote, but that's even worse, considering that he acted consciously.

There is no need of pity in literature and so we needn't be quiet about the futility of Gornfeld's path, but rather make a monument and a scarecrow out of him.

It is for the first time, it seems, that Gornfeld (a very nice person in real life, and educated too) is offering advice. It is certainly interesting to see the positive things that a person with a huge, though negative literary experience can offer us. Albalat's book is entirely based on the analysis of excerpts from prose, discussed from the point of style. All of these excerpts are, of course, known to the French reader and taken from well-known writers.

They offer little to nothing to the Russian reader, as *one cannot learn style from translations.*

Gornfeld understands this when he says that "the book will be useful only to those who, first of all, will try to replace Albalat's French references and juxtapositions with corresponding excerpts and examples from Russian literature."

This kind of substitution should have been done obviously by the editor (as it was done, for example, on page 138, where an original excerpt was substituted with an excerpt from Turgenev), but to burden the reader who is unprepared with this task means to consciously turn the book into something completely useless. The book itself is far from being first-rate.

The author holds the view that laws and even rules of style don't change, i.e. he thinks that people used to write identically, and if they wrote differently, they must have been wrong.

So it turns out that one ought to (always) avoid "repetitions of words," although there is never a shortage of such words in the works of the best writers.

If the reader of Albalat's book starts studying literature, he will find out that repetitions are the rule for the Bible, the *Kalevala*, the Russian so-called folk creativity, as well as for Gogol and Tolstoy who used them rather consciously and widely.

But Albalat is not daunted by this. On page 94 he corrects Racine, Richardson, Cervantes and Sophocles.

In another place Albalat writes: "It is clear, for example, that one ought to go straight to the point and avoid digressions." And yet, Byron's *Don Juan* is full of them. In *Gil Blas* [and also *Don Quixote*—V.S.] the digressive episodes take as much space as the main content. The Russian reader can add to this list, of course, Pushkin's *Eugene Onegin*, but Albalat is not deterred at all, as vulgarity can never be taken by surprise (see *Russkoe Bogatstvo*). He says: a genius allows himself liberties forbidden to common mortals.

What a stupendous idea, since almost all the authors cited by the reputable Frenchman are geniuses. And so, let us write a "decree on liberties" instead of a poetics. Let's note, in the meantime: some of the decrees of the reputable Frenchman are right and speak of the fact that, after all, he was not born in the country where *Vestnik Yevropy* was published. But they appear more as *quackery*, as isolated cases. The success of Homeric descriptions can be possibly explained by his skillful handling of "incidental details." The images that seem successful to Albalat are usually based on the realization of a metaphor, and so on. As it stands, all of the excerpts given merely as landmarks are of no use. Let me conclude. *A Literary Primer* is useless in the way that it is presented by Gornfeld ("to the unprepared reader"), i.e. with translated examples from unknown writers.

If, however, it were equipped with Russian examples (which the editor can accomplish in the second edition of the book), it would turn into an inimitable guide for anyone who wants to learn how to write as they wrote in *Vestnik Yevropy* and *Russkoe Bogatstvo*.

A REVIEW OF THIS BOOK

In my belletristic works I have often written about myself and was the hero of my books. Writers often project themselves and speak through their heroes. This might seem like putting a little greasepaint on, but it strongly affects the work. Because Nekhlyudov and Levin are not Tolstoy.

When we begin to write and portray the hero, when we endow him with an appearance, dress, epigrams, a biography, the hero becomes alive, like a painting that comes to life in a story (which I have fused with others). The hero becomes alive and is further constructed, separated by the material. He separates from the writer, unburdens his responsibility and expresses that political nonsense, which can sometimes be transposed with inspiration. The hero is made from material; he is comprised of material as a library is comprised of books.

Lev Tolstoy has a relatively bad piece of prose called "A Dream." Sreznevsky did some research on this work.

"A Dream" is written in the style of a prose poem. Lev Nikolaevich wanted to publish it and he sent it to the publisher under someone else's name—he presented it as the first literary attempt of Natalia Petrovna Okhotnitskaya. Okhotnitskaya existed, of course, as an author, but she was invented by Lev Nikolaevich.

Okhotnitskaya's work was defective. Then Lev Nikolaevich wanted to insert "A Dream" into *War and Peace* and tried to link it to Pierre, but it didn't work. Then he wanted to link it to Nikolai Rostov, but that didn't work either. The changes for transferring the excerpt into the novel consisted of merely switching from the first personal pronoun to the third: it was not "I saw" but "he saw." Thus, the same piece was going to enter the biographies of different people, which means that these people are nonexistent. They are just composed of this material. Although, in the end, none of them dreamed this dream, but we see this transfer of catchwords from hero to hero in any play. This is particularly characteristic of Dostoevsky, though Dostoevsky didn't really write plays. The catchwords are spread out among the speakers and Dostoevsky demarcated their places so that the speakers wouldn't confuse each other. His heroes are fixed spatially because they are not characterized. When a play is staged in a province, they conglomerate the catchwords, densify the roles and generally produce what Viktor Zhirmunsky calls the unity of a work and the unity of a type—a legend.

When Tolstoy was reading *The Power of Darkness* in the Maly Theater, he read badly, shying away from the blunt expressions and saying that they could be removed:

> It was obvious that Lev Nikolaevich speeded up in the parts of the play that abounded in vulgar popular expressions. When reading the conversation about the dug out holes, the audience noticed that the author was feeling ill at ease. After reading a certain phrase, L.N. said that the phrase is crossed out as it may shock some of the ladies.

This is a common phenomenon: an author can write anything, but it might be impossible for him to read it out loud.

At the end of the reading they started discussing the production and actors. Lev Nikolaevich described Mitrich as a deep-voiced, wide-mouthed peasant. In the meantime, this role was going to be played by Nikolai Muzil who had the opposite physique. And those who had gathered felt somewhat awkward.[46]

So, you see, whatever seems to be self-explanatory in the novel, i.e. that the specific features of the hero correspond with his "character," it does not transfer onto *the stage* at all and it often turns out that it's also possible to have a hero with a different physique and who fits the work even better.

Hence I do not feel guilty for always writing in first person, especially when it is obvious from what I have just written that, while I write in first person, I don't write about myself.

Besides, *Viktor Shklovsky* about whom I am writing is apparently not quite me, and had we met and started up a conversation, we might even have some misunderstandings.

Mitrich has different physical features, while I am thirty-four years old and have the pyknic body type. But if I start to characterize myself again, it will turn into a literary work.

So what is it that I consider to be important in my literary, non-theoretical work?

It is the sensation of the disunity of forms and the free treatment of those forms.

The idea of the cohesion of a literary work is replaced with the sensation of the value of a separate piece. I am more interested in the contradictions than in the cohesion of the pieces.

---

46   Pavel Pchelnikov, *O Tolstom* [*About Tolstoy*], 1909.

So this is evidently necessary for today's momentum of literary development, and this peculiarity of mine has not been left out of literature, but has been introduced into literature by me.

I began writing from an early age. The first pamphlet that I published was titled "The Resurrection of the Word." It was about transrational language (*zaum*), but it appeared in the theology section of the bookstore as the typesetter had used an antique typeface for the heading.

Then I befriended Lev Yakubinsky and worked with Osip Brik already as a theorist.

I came to belletristic writing (if I am to be called a belletrist) through the newspaper *Zhizn Iskusstva* (*The Life of Art*). I was a member of the editorial board. Mikhail Kuzmin worked there before me and Hayk Adonts came after me. The newspaper had a very small circulation and the copies were frozen-glued to the fences with water, as there was no flour for making real glue.

I was publishing my theoretical articles and feuilletons in that newspaper. Then Zinovi Grzhebin commissioned me to write an autobiographical book and was paying some thousands per month.

I wrote a small book called *Revolution and the Front.*

A Sentimental Journey was written in Finland in ten days, I think, as I needed the money very much. This doesn't mean that I can write a book every ten days but that apparently it was ready and came around in the wake of those ten days.

Zoo was written in Berlin and was originally conceived as something hastily put together. I wanted to give some descriptions of writers and insert samples of their works, and to give Zinovi Grzhebin his trademark.

I had several descriptions in the original version of the book, which I later threw out. They were all very offensive. I had an article there on the Smenovekhovtsy[47] and a description of the director of Helikon publishing, Abram Vishnyak.

Even now I can hardly contain myself from saying a few unpleasant things about him.

But at the same time I had a completely different theme in mind: I needed a motive for tying several disconnected pieces together.

I introduced the theme of interdiction against writing about love, and this interdiction brought autobiographical elements, the theme of love into the book, and when I placed the pieces of the already complete book on the parquet floor and sat down to glue the pieces together, it turned out to be a different book, not the one I had originally set out to write.

I had to revise some parts, and, generally speaking, the book was rashly written and one shouldn't read it out loud. The book is better than its original intention.

Then I wrote a book completely incomprehensible to me called *Third Factory*.

I wanted to capitulate in it to time, and what is more, to capitulate by transferring my troops to the other side. To recognize contemporaneity. Apparently my voice didn't turn out as such. Or the material on the village and the material on my unsettled life inserted into the book stuck out, its arrangement turned out not as intended, and people were offended by it. Books are not usually written to be liked, and books are not only written but they take place, they happen. Books distract

---

47   A nationalist movement in the Russian émigré community that began shortly after the publication of the journal *Smena vekh* (*Change of Signs*) in Prague in 1920. The members of the group, some of them with strongly anti-Communist convictions, nevertheless collaborated with the Bolshevik government believing that the revolution was a Russian national process leading toward the restoration of Russia as a great power with a universal mission.

the author from his intention. I am not trying to justify myself, I am simply stating a fact. Now I write notebooks.

I turn works into scrap by not connecting them artificially. My conviction is that the old form—the form of the personal fate, the stringing of events onto a glued hero is not useful today. The new form, which will provisionally consist of the creation of a focus on the material—this new form, the form of the high feuilleton and the newspaper note—does not exist yet.

Journeys, autobiographies, memoirs—these are the surrogate forms of the new pre-literature. No one needs thick novels or epic canvases now. They are like aluminum carts made during a time when one ought to build steel and aluminum cars. The literature of tomorrow will not only be thematically but also formally different from today's literature.

The so-called contemporary literature piled up in complete collections of works should probably be tied into packages. It lives on the memories of another literature, it is being worn out like the imperial theaters. It has become a custom—like wearing a tie.

Whereas I am apparently a writer's writer, not a reader's writer, but I am not rushing anyone.

In the newspaper, where form is unnoticeable, where it bears its true characteristic of craft, I am a writer for everyone. Now I am forced to work in film and that is certainly not literature—it is some other kind of craft. I have been working in film for four years already. I have acquired enough skills so that my head has started to clear up and I have the possibility of taking up literature again.

Coming from literature, I was more demanding in film than any ordinary cinematographer would be, and I brought with me respect for the material.

In my work I try not to unfold a neutral plot against a neutral background, but rather to create a plot—a composition—from the main contradictions of the material itself.

I think that this is beneficial for the cinematographers, otherwise you end up with empty shots, and the people on the screen have nothing to occupy themselves with.

Yes, and on the difficult question—the relationship between the writer and his time.

I will say rather naively: they were demanding Soviet cinematography from filmmakers in my presence. That's how Napoleon ordered his chemists to make a new type of sugar (not from sugar cane).

I became convinced that an assignment coming from outside of art is often beneficial for art.

Cinematography reduced my insularity, made me less complicated and apparently more contemporary. I also see in cinematography how form is created, how something is invented out of contradictions and errors, and how the fixing of an accidental change turns out to be a newly found form. Later on this form can exist independently from the setting in which it was created, even show resistance to that setting, and conserve the material contained in itself. The intersection of an artistic form with a nonliterary system occurs through explosions.

There is no rule of three here, but only reason; the rule of three in science is a lie.

If a person can write a book in ten days, it does not mean that he will be able to write thirty-six books in three hundred and sixty days. There are no simple functional relations here and the problem with swimming pools cannot be solved without differential calculus because the time to drain a vessel depends on the height of the liquid column, which changes.

The old sociological method is based on the rule of three, on a simple functional relation, and it does not properly take into account the resistance of the material. Like old Darwinism, this method is not the absolute truth. It has slightly changed the setting, somewhat changed the organism, but that's erroneous.

Just as erroneous as my former position on the pure, nonliterary system that does not change depending on external factors.

THE JOURNAL AS A LITERARY FORM

ON THE THICK AND THE THIN JOURNALS

Dickens once wanted to create a new prose form—a "super-novel." This new form was going to consist of several novels that intersect one another.

The novels would be published in the form of a journal.

They would be linked by the fact that they were narrated by a company of gentlemen and their servants in the kitchen. The link would be further supported by the premise that the narrators were also the heroes or relatives of the heroes of the novels.

Dickens didn't succeed in writing his "super-novel," however a few fragments did come out of this project, including *The Old Curiosity Shop*.

We can see from this that the novel is not the ultimate or the only literary form that allows for extensive development.

Heine perceived every single one of his collections of poems as a whole and this was not just in the sense of "mood" or some other vague thing, but in the sense of a detailed design of the order of the poems and their dependence on one another.

And it is not the same for the contemporary reader to read Blok's poems in *The Snow Mask* or in the new edition of the book where, following the author's will, the poems are printed in chronological order. We are seeing here a restructuring of the literary form, the focus of which is not on verbal expression. I don't think that the new edition will replace the old one for the reader.

THE JOURNAL-DIARY

The prose writer has often thought about publishing his own journal. It is not so much the need to be alone with one's reader—since the book completely answers that need—as the interest in the journal perceived as a literary form.

At the beginning of journalism, it seemed that "monologic" journals would dominate the field. Indeed, an article placed next to an excerpt from a novel and a chronicle makes a new impression on a person who is used to long-form literature.

Curiously, Heine asked Immermann to insert two pages of any kind of writing into one of his prose works—I think it was *Pictures of Travel*.

It is possible that he needed a combination of styles resembling the Persian "patchwork poems" where Persian and Arabic verses alternate. By inserting someone else's prose into his own, Heine worked, of course, as an artist, but this was a journal device.

THE UNDESCRIBED CLASSICS

The history of the Russian journal is even more obscure and confusing.

Russian journalism has been studied without the consideration of the journal's form. People were only surprised to see colorful fashion drawings in the old thick journals; they were surprised that Pushkin wrote small yellow notes in them. The notes were plucked out of the journals and published separately as collected works where they immediately gained a respectable appearance.

Russian journalists, such as Senkovsky, with a print run of thirty-five thousand copies, are still misunderstood when read outside of their journal.[48]

Instead of exploring the journal form, we merely restate, as something definite, the comments that journalists made to one another in the process of their work.

This is why it is not surprising at all that we despise Senkovsky. It is amazing, though, that we don't consider Orlov a classic—Pushkin praised him, after all.

Biblioteka dlya chtenia is a yet undescribed Russian classic.

THE JOURNAL AS A LITERARY FORM

Political journals get in the way of our perception of the journal as a literary form. But there is a history behind this. Russian censorship was more merciful toward thicker books. Politics had moved into the journal, thickening itself with belletristic prose. Belletristic prose was sometimes used as illustration material and more often as camouflage.

At the same time, the journal was a substitute for the library. If we looked at the regions of distribution, we would easily see that the journals went to the very edges, the farthest corners of the empire.

---

48 Osip Senkovsky (1800-58) was the editor of the popular nineteenth-century Russian literary journal *Biblioteka dlya chtenia* (*Library for Reading*), whose lively and humorous style attracted even those who had never held a book in their hands.

By the way, there is a description of a journal in Panaeva's and Nekrasov's novel *Three Countries of the World* the editorial board of which takes upon itself to not only distribute the journal, but also work on other commissions such as the purchase of furniture and needles, invitation of governesses, etc.

This part of the novel is presented as a pamphlet and is about real incidents. The ploy doesn't work but it is characteristic of its time; it points at the role of the journal to serve as a link between the periphery and the center, to use today's language.

UNDER THE AUTUMN STARS

So, the Russian journal was under a different system of social, economic, and literary influences. Many of those circumstances have disappeared today. The censors treat the journal, the book, and the paper in the same way. The connection between the province and the center is immeasurably better now than in the time of Nekrasov. The journal—and I am talking about the thick journal here—has no basis for its existence in the old form. Even literature is tearing itself away from the journal. If the length of a chapter in Dickens was explained by journalistic conventions, *Rossia* simply rips Ilya Erenburg's novel into two parts for two issues. Gorky is published everywhere in pieces of various length.

The journal can exist now only as a unique literary form. *It must hold interest not only through its separate parts, but also their interconnection.* This is most easily attained in the illustrated journal, which is born on the editorial workbench. The picture and caption form something new, something interconnected. Unfortunately we have very few masters in this "minor" journalistic craft.

Such journals are drawn to the thick journals. They are not very successful—they only get boring.

Meanwhile, it is possible to succeed in the sphere of the really thin journal: the recent example of *Krokodil* (*Crocodile*) can serve as proof.

The situation is worse with regard to thick journals; they aspire to nothing as they are already thick—already great literature. *Zvezda* (*Star*) was launched with this aim—"to restore the century-old tradition of thick journals." It is utterly unclear as to which part of this tradition Zvezda wants to restore.

The literary monthly *Krasnaya Nov* (*Red Virgin Soil*) works a bit less unreservedly, but it is still an old, thick journal with articles (which are printed separately right away) and some works of prose, etc. It is an imitational journal.

It would be interesting to check the issues of this journal in the library to see if they are divisible on the whole. They say that only the belletristic prose is cut up.

LEF is also a thin-thick journal. The good thing about it is that it does not publish everything. Russian journals are unusually tolerant these days. Of course, I am speaking only of literature. They print everything everywhere. You can't differentiate one journal from another. I apologize (like Pushkin in *The Captain's Daughter*) for not analyzing the journals *Molodaya Gvardia* (*Young Guard*) and *Oktyabr* (*October*)—their type hasn't been established yet.

There are no thick journals in the West today. There are only semi-thick politico-artistic journals published by various associations. Only *LEF* and *Na postu* belong to this type.

But we are currently experiencing a crisis of the big literary form. Perhaps we need a new journal, which, by placing different pieces of aesthetic and non-aesthetic material side by side, could illustrate, at least inadvertently, how and from what it is possible to construct works of a new genre.

My article is not programmatic and it does not aspire to be programmatic. It is only a new assignment on the old and the future journal.

STARS CIRCLING AROUND SATELLITES, OR FELLOW TRAVELERS AND THEIR SHADOWS, OR "FIGURES OF INFLUENCE"

Gorky has the following in his *Notes from a Diary*: a person takes off his boot, places it on the floor and says, "Well, go on," and then, "There! You can't go anywhere without me."

Nikolai Tikhonov could have said those words to the poet Grigori Lelevich.

Bezymensky writes in one of his poems: "thought bends its knees." I know why it bends its knees—they bend in parallel fashion—"nerves ... they fall off their feet." That's from Mayakovsky's "A Cloud in Pants." These are all phenomena that obey the laws of nature. Why shouldn't Bezymensky copy Mayakovsky's imagery, if Khodasevich is borrowing his intonation from Pushkin's and Batyushkov's verses, discarding their old words, and filling the voids with substitute material, his own kind of literary scrap type-metal?

The bourgeois writer and proletarian writer both have the right to imitate. Every Russian writer now has his own fellow traveler.

Mayakovsky has Bezymensky. Aseev has Sayanov. Bryusov has Gerasimov. Pilnyak and Chekhov have Libedinsky.

There is a whole theory in the twentieth issue of *Na postu* that acknowledges this fact, but now strives to cast the classics into shadow. A poet's first steps are defined by his teachers. From whom should one inherit the selection of themes and depth of their development? What kinds of rhythm, intonation should one cultivate? These questions are resolved personally and play an important organizing role until the beginner learns to relate critically to the works of his *maître*. For example, the group of young peasant poets called "Pereval" (Pass) discovered the formula of "a visitor's perspective" on the village in Yesenin's work. They adopted his manner of lamenting the old, patriarchal order, presenting general conversations about the hut (without a single reference to the specific work done by the peasant)—all of this has blossomed profusely in their poems. Many young authors perish ingloriously on the way to surpass their teachers. That's why it is very important for the poets of the second summoning to know who guided Bezymensky, Svetlov, Sayanov, Kirsanov, Bagritsky, and others.

There is no doubt that the young poets made wide use of Mayakovsky's and Aseev's formal achievements. Sayanov, Kirsanov, and Ushakov took a prosody course led by the author of "The Black Prince."[49] Bezymensky, Kirsanov, and partly Zharov have made use of Mayakovsky's oratorical voice. The Constructivists developed their own theses and separated from LEF. The recent years have turned Boris Pasternak's work of fifteen years into public property. Ushakov and Dementyev have been very successful in switching over to a more laconic syntax, filling up their calendar with urban images and comparisons that

---

49   Nikolai Aseev's ballad "about the British gold that sank just off the port of Bala-clava in 1854," dedicated to the Russian victory over the British in the Battle of Balaclava during the Crimean War.

are characteristic of the work of the author of *My Sister—Life*.[50] The legacy of Yesenin's lyric poetry is rather insignificant compared to the influences of the leftist masters. It may have affected the work of the Pereval group, but the perspective of their growth is under a big question mark.

The majority of poets of the first summoning have understood early on that you can't arrive at a poem by only studying the contemporaries of the great culture of verse. One should know classical literature well enough to choose for oneself—calmly, rationally—alternate figures of influence. The list expands with each passing year. Tyutchev (disciple: Ushakov), Yazykov (Utkin), Heine (Svetlov), Edgar Allan Poe, and Shevchenko (Bagritsky) have been added to the names of Pushkin and Koltsov. The poets of the second summoning are left with an infinite variety of Russian and world poetry that has been hardly touched by their elder brothers in pen. It is a shame, but it is true—there is no one to follow Nekrasov's muse besides Demyan Bedny. Lyric poets don't notice the mastery of Zhukovsky's or Fet's form. Lermontov didn't inflame any hearts. And what about Hugo, Goethe, Verhaeren? Yes, and we can't pass by Byron—a disciple becomes a true poet only when he surpasses his teacher. To surpass Byron, to utilize the devices of his *Childe Harold's Pilgrimage* to promote a love of life—isn't that a tremendous task?

The only thing that I don't understand in all this is black ingratitude. If a proletarian writer is leaning against Tikhonov, is Tikhonov not supposed to move at all? Tikhonov also wants to grow. It is not his fault if it is convenient for someone to be a shadow of an unchanging subject.

Every living writer grows and changes.

---

50   Boris Pasternak's volume of poems on personal journeys, permeated with the tension and promise of the impending October Revolution.

But *Na postu* criticizes writers for this, as if it were a betrayal. Ivanov and Tikhonov have been ruined, they say in *Na postu*.

Arriving late by half an hour, the shadows are, in a way, right in their criticism. The only thing that's not right is when they want to preside over literature. There was an analogous case in history—a shadow got rich and found his owner lying on the ground by his feet. It is a hard and thankless job. I don't advise turning Mayakovsky into a shadow.

It is possible, of course, to change the owner and fill in Pushkin's schemes with one's own words, but literature will die because imitators can't push it forward. So it's best to leave everything as is.

We are witnessing the transfer of culture into the hands of the new class. The writer now feels that his reader has changed. History has reserved a place for proletarian writers. There is no need for them to occupy their place with hats.

In the meantime, only Gastev is sitting in his rightful place of an independent writer. And he too isn't writing.

Proletarian writers need a good school now. They don't need to develop their sound-imitating abilities and the introduction of slogans into literature such as: "Nowhere but in Mosselprom," while proletarian poetry is in *Oktyabr*.

I just can't understand why Mayakovsky is a fellow traveler, while Utkin is a guide. And I don't understand how Tikhonov turned out to be a fellow traveler when he didn't write a single line before the revolution. And now, here is a piece of advice: safeguard the sources of light. Make your own light, without the help of influential figures. There is no need to go after old literature like a cyclist riding after a tramcar. You have the electricity!

THE FIGHT FOR FORM

Snowy Tibet has its own theater.

The plays for this theater are written by a Buddhist monk. But in most of the plays rabidly spinning priests in wide cloaks and black hats intrude upon the stage amid the Buddhist masks.

The fact is that before Buddhism, people in Tibet had another religion—Shamanism. The priests spinning in the Buddhist play are shamans similar to the shamans of our Siberian tribes.

How were they preserved in the religious plays of another, a conquering religion?

There is a legend about a Buddhist monk who dressed as a Shamanic priest and partook in their dances in order to assassinate the chief who revolted against Buddhism.

Under this pretext, the old shamans were allowed to stay. Our art abounds in shamanic dances.

Meyerhold's *The Government Inspector*, with its exquisite furniture and its exquisitely dressed woman, is a shamanic dance. Those who enjoy the dance, lie to themselves saying that they are not watching the dance of the shamans, but the victory over Shamanism. All film scenes with "the decaying bourgeoisie," dancing foxtrot even as they are decaying, all of those scenes are simply foxtrot, but introduced in a pious way.

The old is preserved in new motivations.

Only the most beautiful and exquisitely dressed people are always right on stage. The audience defends the rogue who pleases him the most.

The fight for form should not be a fight to preserve old forms, otherwise we will turn into shamans. As it is, there is an abundance of old forms.

We write stories that open with a landscape, a description of a morning, a description of how the "doors slammed shut," we insert rain into the description, which, according to Tolstoy, could very well stop coming.

We light up the Christmas tree and play the guitar on stage, and we are surprised that it turns out to be reactionary.

We search for new texts for the plays and operas of the future. The reader's interest in memoire literature, journeys, technology tells us that there is an interest in the message, in what we call "information."

Today we have two kinds of literature: translated literature with completely conventional material and Soviet literature, i.e. local literature with a focus on the material, the message.

A part of our literature functions as translated literature. Ilya Erenburg's work and to some extent Marietta Shaginian's literature can be considered as such.

Translated works are perceived by readers outside the meaning of the facts described in them.

The forms of old plot construction are easily applied to this material.

New works and the works of the future need new forms.

It seems to me that future literature ought to be created using the methods of practical language. We must arrive at the precise description of the object. The chief mistake of the contemporary proletarian writer is that he reproduces the old writer's method of work and doesn't try to find his own method of describing the object.

Art changes dialectically in each segment of time. Literature processes another kind of material. Sometimes it is necessary to apply several "methods of work" to the material.

That's the moment of idiosyncratic quoting.

This type of work with "clichés," which have not yet lost their aesthetic meaning but have already lost their connection to reality, can be found among great artists.

There is a scientific opinion today that the *Iliad* was created not by a naïve poet, but a person for whom mythology was only a set of traditional images.

But there are organic epochs that introduce new material into art.

Every class, every strong group selects and creates for itself its own military tactics.

The French Revolution thus created the skirmish line. It is not advantageous for the proletarian writer to do restorative work on old forms.

In the meantime, if someone were to beat an iron sheet and whistle in the backstage, the elicited emotion is always the same. The guitar and the Christmas tree, no matter what you hang on it, will never change. The fight for form is a fight for a new form.

The old form must be studied as one would study a frog. The physiologist does not study the frog in order to learn how to croak. Even bourgeois writers, such as Saltykov-Shchedrin, Leskov, Tolstoy, wrote that the forms of the novel and the story in which they worked didn't satisfy them anymore.

The decline of cultural skills, which is inevitable during a revolution, made the old form an alluring pre-war norm.

The longing for the pre-war life strengthened Shamanism even further.

That's how Italian immigrants in America imported stinking goat cheese. It was a taste of their homeland.

Proletarian art is growing right before our eyes, although we don't always use them—right under our noses—that's more accurate. We don't know yet what kind of art it is and can only determine the time and place in it.

This art evolves with the speed of a cinematic reel projected on the screen by a tired mechanic during the last séance.

Names live for only two years.

Many things are being rediscovered right before our eyes: today they will discover landscape, tomorrow they will notice that they can write about love.

It seems to me that the rapid change of themes and names in proletarian literature is not accidental and it's certainly not evil.

They are simply finishing off dancing the shamanic dances.

One by one, they are trying out the old forms and inventions.

This isn't Tibet, forms here don't last long.

What we are witnessing is not a process of recovery, but a process of trying out the old. After these trials some will hibernate on the images (of decay), but with negative temperatures, while others will slowly move forward. So how should a writer practically approach the question of the form that we need today?

It is advantageous for him, as someone having a direct relation to objects, to introduce technologies into art.

A writer must always strive, first of all, to create precise determinations, be able to describe things.

The contemporary writer ought to know not only the literary craft, but also some other craft in order to process his works through it.

The contemporary writer must have an additional, nonliterary profession. One cannot learn how to write just by writing.

One must learn how to read in a special way—calmly, slowly, unemotionally.

One must acquire knowledge and technical skills. There is a huge gap between scientific achievements and the contemporary writer's knowledge of those achievements.

Meanwhile, the great writers of the past possessed the knowledge of their time.

It is necessary to improve the method of determining things, enhance the consciousness of perception.

Technology and science will change the way we perceive things, will illumine the stock of images. But one must live in technology, and not make occasional raids and steal from it.

Only through such nonliterary work shall we attain the new literary form.

That's how the writer will attain some stability and stop being so transient.

Without this kind of work, the writer only has his shamanic dance and vertigo.

CAPTIONS[51]

You will have to pause the work for another thirty minutes, Comrade Typist! I need to finish discussing something with my reader.

I know what's on his mind. He thinks: "Where is unity in this book?"

Unity, reader, is in the person who is looking at his changing country and building new forms of art so they can convey life. As for the unity of the book—it is often an illusion, just like the unity of a landscape.

Browse through our works, look for a point of view and if you can find it, then there is your unity.

I was unable to find it.

But I would like to tell the reader something else, to have a real conversation with him as I would with a comrade in a foyer. So, let us imagine that we are wearing coats.

---

51 "Captions" and "Firewood" were later included, with minor changes, in *A Hunt for Optimism*.

THE MAN IN THE COAT—COMRADE YEROFEEV

He used to visit me in the editorial office and never took off his coat, since he probably didn't have a jacket or a shirt underneath. He smelled of Lysol, the smell of night shelters, where they protect people from parasites, but aren't concerned that it might be a nuisance. People in the shelters sleep on slippery tarpaulin and the floor is washed with Lysol.

Lysol smells of disaster.

He was already an old man. Later, when I looked him up, it turned out that he was one of the founders of Russian Decadence, and his books, smelling of Lysol, were still around somewhere in boxes in antiquarian shops.

He brought me a vignette cut out from an old magazine and a Christmas card, showing two pigs playing cards.

The caption under the image said: "English Conservatives are staking everything." I was in charge of an illustrated magazine at the time.

"The material is not suitable," I told the man in the coat.

He looked at me in despair and said, "You didn't read the caption."

"You probably have old illustrated magazines in your apartment," I told him. "Arrange them by theme. For example, 'The Red Square twenty years ago,' or '1905,' and so on, and try to sell them. Bring them here, I'll take a look."

I knew as a journalist that almost any photograph could be renewed with a caption. And besides, there had to be some controversial material in those magazines that stopped publishing, but hadn't yet become antiquated.

Indeed, a few days later I got photographs of Lieutenant Schmidt and his crew before the Sevastopol Uprising.

And that's how I came across these photographs from Siam.

While examining them, I was surprised to see that the Siamese troops were dressed in Russian uniforms and high boots, which entirely contradicted their tropical climate. I recalled my childhood and the corner of Basseinaya and Liteinaya, a strange coat of arms on a photograph, and a caption—such and such photographer, the supplier of the King of Siam.

Then I remembered Gorky's apartment and the bronze skull decorated with turquoise and pierced with a three-edged dagger—an artifact from Siam.

But first let me tell you about the Nikolaevsky College of Guard Cadets.

Here is the Mariinsky Theater Square.

The Nikolaevsky College stands on Ofitserskaya Street. It's a red building. There is a flower shop nearby, and the burnt yellow building of the former secret police or its division is in front of it.

Across from the square stands the roofless Litovsky Castle with black slanting traces of soot above its windows. The castle was a prison, which burned during the February Revolution in the wild wind.

They used to make bonfires in the square before the revolution. Only during severe frosts, of course. And the horses, passing by the bonfire, would draw closer to it to keep warm. In fact, I have a feeling that lately the frosts have become milder in Leningrad.

The Nikolaevsky College was not aristocratic. The young cadets were the children of merchants, and the only "grand" presence there was that of the heavy-handed porter in the foyer with yellow sofas.

In 1896, the seventh son of the King of Siam, Prince Chakrabon, was sent here.

HOW CHAKRABON CAME TO
RUSSIA AND WHAT HE SAW

During the tensions between Siam and France over the disputed Mekong region, the King of Siam, having perhaps some kind of future political alliance in mind, sent one of his sons to Russia. The Prince was admitted to the College under the patronage of the Russian Emperor, wore blue trousers and a striped belt, and for the sake of simplicity was considered a Muslim by his peers. They never took him to the court and if he ever saw the Empress, then it was only when she was exiting the castle through a small child's doorway, as if through a hole.

She was usually dressed in a red cloak, and the Winter Palace was painted in the same color to match her cloak.

A FEW LINES ON CHARITY

On Sundays Chakrabon would go to the house of his supplier, who was a Jewish photographer, and read *Faust* with Doré's illustrations,[52] which substituted for the Old Testament in the households of the Jewish intelligentsia.

The photographer had a daughter. Chakrabon would take her on rides in a carriage.

Frost and love. Love! Blessed be your fifteen minutes, which I'm now bestowing upon the Prince of Siam.

Even the horses know that people kiss in carriages in the winter, there—in the back, right behind one's tail.

---

52   While *Faust* is certainly the sort of text that Gustave Doré could have illustrated, there is no evidence that he ever did so. The best-known illustrations of *Faust* were produced by Eugène Delacroix in 1827.

The shadow of a kissing couple traditionally evades sleighs by street lamps.

When the Prince felt the frost on his lips again, he didn't know what to say.

ABOUT THE RUSSIAN EMPIRE—BASED ON RECOLLECTIONS AND OTHER MATERIALS

It was a well-adjusted empire: fish and bread, goose and oil in cisterns crossed it, passing each other without interference and without having the need to clarify their relations.

It was an empire with museums, universities, landscapes, and vast spaces.

The Caucasians were sent to serve in Ukraine, the Crimean Tatars served in Bessarabia.

According to this analogy, they sent the Prince to Kiev.

The cavalry regiment, where Chakrabon served, was stationed near the Kiev Monastery of the Caves.

This is where his love affair began.

THE PRINCE'S LOVE AFFAIR—WRITTEN ACCORDING TO TURGENEV

I am not going to describe the woman. She has been described by Turgenev, and he used to describe women in great detail, as property.

It was spring and there was a ball—a predictable coincidence.

A warm breeze came from the ballroom, most likely from the orchestral helicons. The cold leaves of the hysterical poplars in the garden could have been emanating a scent of human sweat.

A nightingale sang in several voices, hidden, like field artillery behind a veil of smoke.

His head was spinning from the waltz.

Here Chakrabon kissed a Russian woman and, according to the law of the genre, became her husband.

THE NEXT CHAPTER

It was terrifying to be by her side after the wedding—energetic and hot. She was very different from the descriptions in the books. It was as if he had been seized by a fighter of unequal strength. He wanted to move to the corner of the bed and, taking the blanket, sit through the night by the nickel-plated headboard. Or go into the foyer, where his overcoat hung undisturbed by anyone.

But two years went by. The Prince was getting bored. He was serving in the regiment, reading Blok, Balmont, and still getting bored. One morning the French consul came to see him.

"Your Royal Highness," he said, "the King of Siam, your father, has passed away. Being that your elder brothers have also died, we have received the following telegram: 'Your Royal Highness is being summoned back to occupy the ancestral throne.'"

A CHAPTER ON SIAM, WRITTEN BASED ON INFORMATION FROM THE BROCKHAUS ENCYCLOPEDIC DICTIONARY AND RATZEL'S ETHNOGRAPHIC WORK

"The Siamese refer to their country as Mueang Thai, which means 'land of the free,' or Vudra in Burmese. Siam is a kingdom in the central part of Indochina, between the British colonies in the West and French colonies in the East, and it has been drastically losing its lands since 1893"—the Prince read in the fifty-ninth volume of the encyclopedia, which he purposely took with him on the ship. The King of Siam has three hundred elephants. And forty elephants are more than enough to be happy.

His palace is very different from the Winter Palace. It sits on stilts, with a swarm of disorderly rooms and a rattling crystal bed.

The wives are dressed like bayadères.

Natasha was terrified when they put her in the hallway with the other wives.

There was a fat Chinese man in the hallway.

Natasha should have remembered the lines from Pushkin— "Where the key of the sullen eunuch keeps …"[53]

Natasha was crying at first.

Chakrabon asked her, "Do you want me to build a separate palace for you with twenty rooms and a kitchen?"

THE END OF NATASHA, THE TURGENEVIAN WOMAN, AND QUEEN OF SIAM

53   From the early drafts of Pushkin's unfinished work, "An Evening at the Dacha" (1835), which combined poetry and prose and was later incorporated in another unfinished work, "Egyptian Nights" (1835).

"I have been poisoned," she told her husband. "They crushed the glass of an electric bulb and added it to my food. You are the King and probably have the right to sign prescriptions. The Russian Emperor has the right to even receive communion by his own hand. Please hurry and get me some poison. Why didn't we stay in Kiev?"

The King walked in front of the army at her funeral.

The soldiers were dressed in khaki *gymnastiorkas*, breeches, and visorless caps.[54] The Cambodians, Phuang, Stieng, Laotians, Khmers, and Miao all marched in step.

It sounded as if they were hitting the ground with enormous bundles of dry twigs. A Russian general would have easily let them pass through. The complexion of the soldiers would have signaled to him that they were returning from encampment.

The elephants, with their dark merging drone, followed behind.

The coffin was drowning in flowers, according to the foreigners observing from their balconies.

"Left, left," the instructors quietly counted.

The sticks were hitting the drums, as they bounced against the drummers' knees.

The flutes were calling the deceased to courage.

They placed a pair of stone elephants with raised trunks on Natasha's grave. The elephants were holding up a crown with their trunks.

I had seen the photograph of this grave. It was surrounded by rows of troops in Russian uniforms. The photograph was displayed in a vitrine on the corner of Liteinaya and Baseinaya (now renamed after Nekrasov). That's the photograph the copy

---

54   The uniform of the Russian infantry, which incorporated a military version of the traditional Russian pull-over shirt-tunic called the *gymnastiorka*, trousers with a semi-breeches type cut, and a visored cap. The visorless cap was usually worn in the navy.

of which Yerofeev, the man who smelled of Lysol, gave me at the Palace of Labor.

The photographs had appeared in the different issues of *Niva*.

THE END, BASED ON A PHOTOGRAPH IN A STEREOSCOPE

I know that Chakrabon is still alive and lives in Siam, and since I have had the occasion to travel to the East, I can tell you how Chakrabon learned about the October Revolution.

NOVEMBER IN SIAM

The rice plants had already risen to the water's surface in the swamps of Lake Togesan. The peasants were paddling their flat-bottomed boats through the rice beds. They were bending the stalks over the side of the boat and beating the kernels with sticks, as children play with nettles in Russia. The kernels would sprinkle into the boat.

In the mountains, the peasants were hunting for manure and bats.

The King was in his palace. The door opened without a knock and someone's back was pushed in and turned to the side, letting in the French Resident.

I should mention that the King of Siam spoke only Russian.

"We didn't want to disturb you until the customary period of mourning was over," said the Frenchman hurriedly, without pausing, "but Russia's treacherous withdrawal from the Allied forces compels us to recruit an auxiliary corps from the eighteen tribes that are at your Imperial Highness's disposal."

"… but Russia's treacherous withdrawal," the man in naval uniform was quickly translating into Russian.

ABOUT THE TELEGRAPH IN THE EAST

The telegraph in the East is connected by low iron towers that split at the bottom. It looks like a fence. And the towers look like gossipers. Telegrams get saturated with rumors as they travel along the wires.

I received a telegram in Northern Persia via India that read: "The famous Bolshevik Maksim Gorky was killed by Zinoviev when leaving the Chinizelli Circus. VIKZHEL[55] is protesting."

Imagine this telegram in the hands of Prince Chakrabon.

Or better yet, imagine that you have moved from Moscow to the moon and that it's stifling there. And then you find out suddenly there, on the moon, that you have been forbidden forever to return to Moscow and that they have rented your apartment to someone else. Since nobody has had the chance to read the Bible or the history of Russia cut up into narrow strips and mixed with the morning paper, I can't convey the impression of reading the October telegrams in the East.

The shadows reappeared in the garden again and the sunlight was not so direct when Chakrabon finished reading the last telegram.

The officer was rolling up the telegrams into neat scrolls with the carelessness of a person, who has failed an exam and is putting on his coat in the foyer.

---

55   Abbreviation for the All-Russian Executive Committee of the Railway Workers' Union.

The lieutenant went out into the garden. The garden was in a stereoscope; it was spacious but unreal. The feathers of the palm trees demonstratively signaled the foreground.

What is this like?

Dust that hangs in the air and has no weight.

Pity.

A person who walks on a road overgrown with grass, singing to himself and not realizing that he is singing.

That's what a writer is like.

A song that one absentmindedly sings to oneself.

A god who created the world in haste, in six days, and who is glad that the seventh is Sunday.

FIREWOOD

A CONVERSATION BY THE PRISON GATES

Were they always this heavy?

By the time you get the logs, fetch them home somehow, and carry them upstairs, you don't feel like heating up the stove anymore.

There is a man who helps me with the logs. He's a nice man, he's very generous—we live on the fifth floor. But I am afraid.

My husband, who was Polish, passed away many years ago. My son went off to Warsaw. "I'll write, mama," he told me. But he never does. I live with my daughter-in-law, she is like a daughter to me.

Since there was always a cold draft from under the door of the empty room, we took a tenant.

Georgi Sigizmundovich is Polish too, but he doesn't speak the language. He is a short man, only comes up to my shoulder. He lived with us for a while. But there was still a cold draft from under his door.

"You should keep the stove burning through the night," I told him. "The stove doesn't keep the heat, you'll catch a cold."

"I have healthy lungs," he said, "I can do without."

I got up one morning, and my daughter, you know, she usually sleeps on the stove. I went into the kitchen. They were right

137

there on the stove together, the tenant and my daughter, covered with his coat. His officer's breeches were hanging on the chair. I was really upset. So that's the kind of lungs you have, I thought. I didn't say anything to them. I just started selling the merchandise by myself in the market. I have many things to sell. The tenant started calling me "mamenka."[56] And we lived quietly like that.

It was my husband's death anniversary, and I decided to visit his grave at the Smolensky cemetary. I got up in the morning and started geting dressed in warmer clothes. The tenant found out.

"We'll go with you, mamasha," he says.

It's peaceful in the cemetery. I am standing by the grave. It's cold. I can't even bring myself to cry.

My daughter takes out a piece of paper. She sprinkles some powder on her palm and eats it.

I ask her—what's that?

"These, mamasha, are pills for the heart," Georgi Sigizmundovich instantly replies. "The feldsher at work gave them to me. We are going through difficult times, the blockade, and people don't have any food to share with others. So people eat this powder. You eat it and it makes you happy. I have some for you too, if you want."

I ate the powder.

We left.

I walked ahead. They'll probably start kissing, I thought—I didn't want to get in the way.

Then I heard my daughter saying: "Why isn't she falling?"

"In a second," replied the tenant, and I heard a clicking sound behind my back. I turned around and saw him shooting at me with a revolver. He misfired.

---

56   An affectionate and old-fashioned diminutive form for "mother." *Mamasha* is another diminutive for "mother" that has a more derisive undertone.

I jumped at him. I wanted to squash him into the snow. And without turning the revolver, he hit me straight on my forehead with the barrel. But that's good because I would've been dead had he hit me with the handle, even though he's a weak man. I fell to the ground, screaming, and the blood was pouring into my eyes. I tried to cover the wound with snow, but all I was grabbing was sand. I could hear them running away, my daughter running and screaming. Some workers who were painting crosses caught them. They dragged them back to where I was.

They were panicked and all they could say was "mamasha." The workers beat Georgi Sigizmundovich badly. They kept pushing his head into the pool of blood and he kept saying: "I'm sorry." They gave him a sled and told him: "Since *you* tried to killed her, *you* take her to the hospital."

I was taken to the hospital and the doctors were shocked, because as it turns out, I had been given a dose of strychnine. I was ill for some time and then I recovered. I returned home. Lived alone for a while.

It's cold. It blows from under the door. I am walking along the street one day. A sleigh comes up to me, with a convoy guard and next to him is a woman lying with her face down and her feet kicking up in the air. She is wearing my stockings.

"What's the matter with you, dear?"

"He doesn't love me, mamasha, so I took poison."

I got in the sleigh with her and we rode to the prison hospital. She got medical treatment and it turned out that she was pregnant.

They don't keep pregnant women in the prison here because it's too crowded. So I took her and brought her home. Georgi Sigizmundovich is still in prison. He has a nice handwriting, and he is a meticulous man. He works as a clerk there, does some office work. I didn't complain about him too much in the court.

They let him out on Sundays. He came once to visit us, stood by the gates. Then started helping with the logs, and now we drink tea together on Sundays.

My son still hasn't written to me from Warsaw.

The firewood there must be cheaper!

CINEMA

SOMETHING LIKE A DECLARATION

NUMA POMPILIUS

There is an ancient Roman legend recorded by Livy, I think.

The gods negotiate with Numa Pompilius on the nature of sacrifice that would please them (Livy's style of writing). The gods want human sacrifice. Numa Pompilius pretends not to understand them. "We ask for something human," the gods say. Numa Pompilius offers them a lock of human hair. "We are talking about something that is alive," the Gods insist. Numa Pompilius offers them two live fish. "We are asking for something round, we want heads," the gods say. Numa Pompilius offers them a head of garlic.

And so, the gods get a completely useless assortment of things.

The scriptwriters and Glavpolitprosvet[57] are having somewhat similar conversations today.

Glavpolitprosvet wants something alive and human, based on live material, something that will express class relations.

The scriptwriters offer fish, garlic, and captions.

The conversations are long and painful.

---

57   The Main Committee on Political Enlightenment, established in 1920 as an agency of the People's Commissariat of Education (Narkompros), was responsible for organizing and carrying out the political education of adults in the Soviet Union.

WINGS OF A SERF

There was a script titled *Wings of a Serf.* It described how a man flew during the reign of Ivan the Terrible and what followed from it. Ivan the Terrible in this script was taken from Count Aleksei Tolstoy's historical novel *Prince Serebriany.*

Glavpolitprosvet wanted something else. We suddenly realized that we shouldn't fool the gods and that we shouldn't follow the pseudo-classical tradition of Numa Pompilius. The guilty party in this violation of tradition was the artist Leonidov from the Moscow Art Theater. He announced that it was impossible to play an Ivan the Terrible who was roaring and killing people. Then we decided to cast Ivan the Terrible based on real historical material. We recalled that Ivan the Terrible owned the first mechanized flax mill in Russia established by the Englishman Harvey, that he competed with Novgorod in the manufacture of flax, that not only did he kill but also traded and even created a monopoly of flax production. And as soon as we introduced real, historical, nontraditional material, the script started to fall into place. It became clear where the wings of the serf came from, because you can't fly without machinery, whereas Ivan the Terrible's weapon smithies and mechanized factories could make machinery. Now the queen also had to be involved, since she managed the white treasury (flax production).

Ivan the Terrible finally had a role to play and the film director, Yuri Tarich, was able to rework the script so that the actor and the film factory were content.

MONTPENSIER CANDY

What shocked me when I first came to the film factory was the smell of Montpensier candy.

The thing is that strips of film are glued together with pear spirit and, of course, pear spirit smells of caramel.

This smell penetrates into the film director's room and script-writer's head.

The smell of Montpensier candy in Soviet cinematography can be eliminated only with the introduction of real, historical material.

The political demand of the day partly coincides with the artistic demand.

The issue here is not to evade these assignments but rather to use them artistically.

We are now placing a bet on *Wings of a Serf*—a film without Montpensier candy, garlic, fish, or human hair.

It seems to us that we have been successful in reworking the material in the script.

Cinema searches for new material that is exotic, national, it searches for new shots. Meanwhile the history of trade and the history of culture, even the history of trousers, if we take it scientifically, can give more material to cinematography than all the Dorothy Vernons taken together.

FIVE FEUILLETONS ON EISENSTEIN

FIRST FEUILLETON

The artist has certain freedoms regarding material from everyday life: the freedom to select, the freedom to change, and the freedom to reject. The directors of the film *Ninth of January* didn't use any of these. They say the film cost several hundreds of thousands of rubles—that's very sad indeed, and it's a great shame. Apart from a few crowd scenes, the film is consistently bad ... The fault of the directors is that they didn't use their freedoms. They took everything in a row, filmed everything as it was, and this, of course, resulted in something that never was, because you can't transmit the revolution in a boring way.

Eisenstein is a colossal master; he has used his freedoms. His first achievement in *Battleship Potyomkin* was that he narrowed the topic, skillfully selected the moments, didn't take 1905 as a whole, but focused only on the battleship and took only the steps out of entire Odessa. The revolt was filmed cleverly, large-scale, in typical Eisensteinian fashion, with a good close-up, against a white backdrop, and not against aesthetic black velvet.

The revolt of "Potyomkin" was unsuccessful. The battleship and the shore could not help one another. The disorganized revolt of the sailors came to a dead end in Constanța. But Eisenstein was able to find heroic moments in the revolt and show the pathos of the battleship's passage through the Admiralty Squadron.

There is a correct distance between Eisenstein's film and history. And Eisenstein, like "Potyomkin" with its revolutionary flag, passed through history, gave shape to matter, and raised the flag: "Join us!" The film is a complete success. It holds the viewer's attention. It is interesting. Everything in it is grandiose.

SECOND FEUILLETON

The big themes haven't yet reached the land of the Rus.

We can still talk about whether Eisenstein is a genius, and whether Russian cinematography is genius too. But Eisenstein's genius is not at stake here. The issue rather is how to direct Russian cinematography. We have lost our freedom—our hands are tied. We are trying to create commercially profitable films; we show nude women in *The Minaret of Death* and assert that it's not pornography, but a scenery film.

In order to move Soviet cinematography in the right direction, people must believe in the genius of our time, they must understand that Eisenstein didn't just appear out of thin air. Eisenstein is the logical conclusion of Left Front's work. Maybe Eisenstein should be reproached for standing in second place or maybe even at the end and not the forefront of his movement. But in order for Eisenstein to even exist, there had to be Kuleshov with his conscious approach to film material. There had to be the Kino-Eyes, Dziga Vertov, the Constructivists, and the birth of the concept of plotless cinema.

It is easy to recognize Eisenstein's genius, because one man's genius is not so offensive. You can give a genius film stock, Tisse for a cameraman, and a big salary, but it's harder to recognize the genius of the time that we live in. Soviet cinematography must not flow with the current; it must invent and fight for the existence of film culture. The Protazanovs, Yegorovs, Aleinikovs are all very good, but they are worthless from the point of view of orientation.

THIRD FEUILLETON

What can Eisenstein do, and what can't he do?

He obviously knows how to handle objects.

The objects are shown marvelously in his work: the battleship really becomes the hero of the film. The cannons, their movements, the masts, the steps—all are acting. But the doctor's pince-nez in Eisenstein plays much better than the doctor himself.

The actors, models—or however they are called on Eisenstein's set—don't work and he somehow doesn't want to work with them either, and this weakens the first part of the film. Sometimes Eisenstein succeeds in portraying a person—that happens when he perceives the character as a quote, as an object, and casts in a standard way. Barsky (the Captain of "Potyomkin") is great in that sense; he is as good as a cannon. The people on the steps are even better, but the steps are the best of all.

The steps are the plot. Parts of the landing play the role of deferment, and the steps, on which the carriage with the baby rolls slowing down, picking up speed, are organized according to the kinship laws of Aristotle's *Poetics* (Chapter 14). The *peripeteia* of the drama is born out of this new form. But Eisenstein doesn't succeed in the escape scene, the moment when people are running in different directions.

Some things were left underdeveloped. The projector, for example. The daybreak scene is really good, but it's too aesthetic. Tisse is a very talented man, but his dawn is too artistic—it belongs in a different film. This is a perfect example of how little material matters and how much depends on the director who manipulates the material. All you need to do is compare the steps in Eisenstein with the steps in Granovsky: the steps are the same and the cameraman is the same, but the outcome is different.

FOURTH FEUILLETON

Pushkin's vocabulary is not rich in new words because he is the last writer of his generation. The new forms had already been created by his time, he simply perfected them, but Pushkin had his own vocabulary and rhythm—the forms would become quasi-unconscious, retreat from the visible field of the perceiving reader—and therein lies Pushkin's genius.

In *Potyomkin*, Eisenstein's signature techniques such as montage, camera angles, cinematic punctuation (dissolves, diaphragms), all are infinitely less visible than in *The Strike*. There are only two dissolves in the entire film, and both are semantically justified: the steps instantly filling with people, and the deck of the battleship instantly emptying.

The dissolves economize the exposition of the scenes and aren't perceived as a cinematic trick. The film is brilliant because the objects in it are not cluttered. I think that the device of economy has been consciously observed here—it unifies the action.

There are only a few scenes that remain from the old Eisenstein: the commander being wrapped in the tarpaulin—a completely unnecessary mess right out of *The Strike*. The tarpaulin worked well on its own, when it swelled in the wind. There was no need of touching it further. And there was no need of killing Vakulinchuk so gracefully either. Besides, he should have been killed earlier, because if he is killed when the sailors have already won and most of the officers have been killed, his death cannot be perceived to be "by the hands of the executioners."

FIFTH FEUILLETON

Was it necessary to have the color red—the flag, raised on the mast of the battleship? I think it was. An artistic work, and particularly a cinematic work, deals with semantic dimensions, and red is a material in the theme of 1905. The artist shouldn't be blamed that during screenings people applaud the revolution and not him per se.

There is a very visible red flag above the Kremlin. But people walking on the street don't applaud it.

Eisenstein painted the flag boldly, but he had a right to that color.

The fear of boldness, the fear of simple, perceptible effects in art is vulgar. Painting the flag once in the film gets the point across. It's done by the real hand of a daring person.

ON CINEMATIC LANGUAGE

Sometimes you can check yourself on foreign films.

I thought of this because I saw a shot in *A Woman of Paris*, which I vainly offered up to anyone who passed through cinematography.

The shot is the following: a woman stands on the station platform and the lights of the approaching train run across her body.

Lev Vladimirovich Kuleshov and I wrote this scene in a script about a year ago. There are, of course, many such scenes in it. The thing is that organic substances often don't withstand complex chemical processing. They are ground down.

At the bottom of art, like a nest of fermentation, lies cheerfulness.

It is difficult to preserve it, difficult to explain it to a non-specialist.

Inventiveness needs an audience; we are wasting away the cheerfulness of our creators. The "shots" or the angles are not the issue here.

Shots can be easily worked out.

The issue is art.

Films can be produced cheaply, and they can be produced expensively.

We are forced to produce them cheaply in our country.

But cinematography requires money.

Soviet comedy is unsuccessful.

I cannot imagine when it will succeed.

Because in order to succeed, it must pass several committees and it must make them laugh. There is a logic in the analysis of invention, but no logic of invention. Committees don't invent. Any script for an action film will be flawed due to artistic, not ideological reasons. We can't have Eccentrism yet. Read what they are writing in Leningrad about the FEKS.[58] All of those writings are as plain as the mooing of a cow in front of locked gates.

No one apparently has a recipe for Soviet comedy film. We know, though, that the rural audience gets Max Linder and his films are successful. Pat and Patashon are successful among the urban audience. Buster Keaton is successful in the newspaper. It's easy to notice how little our viewers get out of Keaton's act judging from the laughter in the hall. They liked the railroad in *Our Hospitality*, and they took Keaton's comical stunts seriously and applauded him as they applaud Harry Piel.

Three Ages is almost completely lost on the viewers. They are interested in the dinosaur and the lion that marvels at his polished nails and they admire Keaton's jumping bouts. They laugh out of respect. But this does not solve the issue.

We can't conclude from this that Soviet viewers don't perceive eccentric comedy. The situation is much more complex. Film operates not through mere images but semantic images. In the process of seeing we perceive depth, spatiality, due to the fact that we have two eyes. The combination of the right and the left

58   Factory of the Eccentric Actor (FEKS), a creative association that existed in Petrograd (Leningrad) between 1922 and 1926. In their Manifesto of Eccentrism, the founding members Grigori Kozintsev, Leonid Trauberg, Sergei Yutkevich, and Georgi Kryzhitsky claimed the call of the auctioneer, street language, the circus poster, the jazz band ("the Negro orchestra"), cinema, and boxing as the "parents" of Eccentric art.

eyesight creates a sensation of magnitude. Film is shot from the point of view of a single eye. And yet we see depth in film. This depth is semantic. We believe in the spatiality of the shot due to the movement in the frame, especially from inside out (toward us)—diagonally.

That is why in cinema they don't use set decorations where nothing moves, or roads that haven't been taken. It is interesting to note that an actor can be replaced with another actor and the audience won't notice the difference if there is no emphasis on the change. But the audience notices that Harry Piel is wearing white gaiters on one roof and no gaiters on the other. That's because the camera is focused on his legs when he is jumping.

And it wouldn't hurt our film directors to know about this either. They use set decorations without manipulating them, and though the decorations are there, the viewer won't notice them on the screen. They are useless. You can't jump off a prop, it just stands there in the background. That's not a set decoration but a cork in the film atelier.

We see cinematic people and actions on the screen the way that they appear to us because we perceive them as such. Cinema resembles most of all Chinese painting. It stands between drawing and words. People moving on the screen are unique hieroglyphs. They are not cinematic images, but rather cinematic words, concepts. Montage is the syntax and etymology of cinematic language. When they showed *Intolerance* for the first time in the Soviet Union, the public couldn't stand Griffith's montage and would leave the séance. Now the public is reading Griffith from an open page.

The conventionality of space, the conventionality of silence, the conventionality of minimalism in cinema—they all have their analogies in language. The cinematographic rule that you can't show how a person sat down at the table, began eating and finished eating, i.e. the rule of selecting from a sequence only the most characteristic part—the sign of the sequence, is the transformation of the cinematic image into a cinematic hieroglyph. That is why it's impossible to say that cinematic language is understandable to everyone. No, it is simply easily assimilated by everyone.

The existence of international centers of production does not contradict this assertion. There is a specific category: US films for Mexico. There used to be films for Russia, too. What we have from world cinematography is extremely peculiar. We are behind in the development of cinematic art by several years. We have mostly seen the work of stage imitators rather than creators. We don't understand the laws of pushing from one cinematic form to another. We don't know any cinematic dialects.

Zoshchenko is successful among the petty-bourgeois audience, however when he has to read in front of the peasantry or workers, he doesn't read "The Lady Aristocrat," but works that are based on the comedy of the situation.

An audience foreign to the literary language can't grasp the comicalness of deviations from language norms. Averchenko was quite popular in China as he employed the humor of the situation, and especially everyday situations, and not language humor.

Cinematic language has its own norms. The incorrect usage of those norms produces the impression of the comical. When they show a *féerie*, film productions from 1914, or *Northern Lights* at the Association of Revolutionary Cinematography (ARK), the audience laughs unreservedly and irresistibly.

Keaton's humor in *Three Ages* is cinematic. He parodies epochal films such as *Intolerance* and *The Birth of a Nation*. The film in itself is not comical; the comedy lies *between* the films. For example, the trees that play the role of prehistoric catapults are comical. So are the awkwardness of parallelisms and the intrusion of one style into the other. The historical drama (chariot racing) is intersected by an English drama (sled-dog racing)—when perceived, the inconsistency creates a comical impression. Taking the dog out of the rear box is associated with taking out a spare tire. This association is not a given for the Soviet viewer. The Negro men in the film are exotic for us. For Americans they are both exotic and ordinary—the divination bones are exotic, Negro men playing bones are ordinary. The clash of perspectives is comical. Then the film proceeds with a play on everyday activities that we don't quite follow either. The consequences of Prohibition and the football game are not funny because we don't know anything about the dry law or the rules of the game. In other words, the whole film needs a *translation*.

A VOICE FROM BEHIND THE SCRIPTS

It is hard to talk to scriptwriters. You realize that their situation is desperate.

They are undermined by three different court instances. They are responsible not only for themselves, but also the place where the scripts are being used.

It's true, there are new currents. But do you know what the light of an extinguished star is?

When an unfortunate star is extinguished in the sky, its light still reaches us for years and even decades.

The same happens in cinematography.

Scriptwriters say: "We were assigned to write a script about the village, about the Orient, now it's about history."

Meanwhile, filmmaking is a long process—one needs to have a script, choose a film director, build set decorations, sometimes even organize an expedition. More than half a year passes. The star of the project has already extinguished, while its light and different partisan films keep pouring in.

The scriptwriters, who have gained speed, can't stop their waffle irons and keep on writing.

Art bureaus spoil piles of scripts, and I can say much more that is not amusing.

So what is the matter?

First of all, it is artistic integrity. People must understand that there can be no directives in art, that strict compliance with directives has always been a form of sabotage.

One must stop listening to the sighs of Glavpolitprosvet.

Scripts must be written based on a social commission and not for an imaginary commissioner.

Then we will overcome the pattern of seasonal scriptwriters, and the scriptwriter will no longer shoot with scripts as if they were pellets hoping that one of them will hit the target.

I and some of my comrades, who are bitterly criticized by cinematographers for being "contaminated with literature," read hundreds of scripts.

The brain begins to form some sort of a crust.

We are no more contaminated with literature than a tramcar with electricity.

Yes, one should speak in the first person.

I commit myself to sharing my experience, brought from my own craft, with my scriptwriter comrades.

I take a script, read it, and ask myself: "What is the invention here? What is the novelty for which we must pay? Is there a new type of hero? Does it have another kind of denouement? A possibility to apply new material?"

As it often happens, I have a historical script in front of me now.

I read about Anna Ioannovna, Anna Leopoldovna, Aleksandr Lyapunov. I know all of this from book extracts (you pay seventy-five kopeks per extract).

If the script is about the village, then I read about wealthy peasants, middle peasants, poor peasants, and about everything else that the newspapers cover in a much better way.

Now all the scripts include flogging as it was customary during serfdom. The flogging scene is not unexpected for the viewer and it is rather questionable in terms of ideology.

The portrayal of sadism on the screen is sadism in itself.

I don't believe that we need bare women's backs full of scars for agitation. Scripts howl monotonously, even more monotonously than packs of wolves.

"You couldn't depict her beauty, so you decorated her," a teacher once said to a painter, who had painted Helen clad in rich adornments. This was in Greece.

I see the same ineptness in us. Scriptwriters make use of all kinds of material instead of doing their work. They are trying to sell an antiquities shop. This happens in every film factory.

Scriptwriters can't stop once they begin quoting from history textbooks.

If there is no uprising scene then a scriptwriter has nothing to work with.

A script on the revolution must necessarily include Father Gapon, January 9, the provocation, the 1905 pogrom against Jews, and two revolutionaries—a member of the intelligentsia and a worker. I just copied this from one of the scripts.

What's happening is a wild extermination of themes.

Themes are being strangled, as though a weasel has broken into the chicken coup. It is pogrom, not work.

There are strange conversations going on in film factories: "Syphilis?—No, we've already shown syphilis." A total extermination of themes! We need to learn not so much how to preserve themes as how to break free from them. How to transform material into constructions.

POETRY AND PROSE IN
CINEMATOGRAPHY

Poetry and prose are not sharply differentiated from each other in verbal art. Prose scholars have often found rhythmic segments—the recurrence of the same phraseological construction—in a work of prose. Tadeusz Zelinsky has interesting studies on rhythm in oratorical speech. Boris Eichenbaum has done much work on rhythm in pure prose intended for reading rather than recitation, although it is true that he didn't pursue his analysis in a systematic way. So in the analysis of rhythm, the boundary between poetry and prose has not become any clearer, but on the contrary—more convoluted.

Perhaps the distinction between poetry and prose does not reside in rhythm alone. The more we study a work of art, the deeper we penetrate into the fundamental unity of its laws. The separate constructive aspects of an art phenomenon are differentiated from one another qualitatively, but their qualitative difference rests on a quantitative base, and we can imperceptibly pass from one realm to the other. The basic construction of plot is reduced to the arrangement of semantic elements. We take two contradictory everyday life situations and resolve them with a third one, or we take two semantic elements and create a parallelism, or we take several semantic elements and arrange them in a stepped order. But the typical foundation of plot is the *fabula*, an everyday life situation, though the everyday life situation is only a particular instance of semantic construction, and we can create a mystery novel out of any novel not by changing the *fabula* but merely by rearranging its constituent parts: by moving the end to the beginning, or a more complex rearrangement of the parts. This is how Pushkin's "The Snowstorm" and "The Shot" are constructed. So, the elements that may be called everyday life elements, i.e. semantic elements, and the purely formal aspects can replace one another and transition from one to the other.

A prose work in its plot construction, in its main composition, is based chiefly on a combination of everyday life situations. This is how we resolve a situation in a work of prose: a person must speak, but he cannot, so another person speaks on his behalf. For example, in *The Captain's Daughter* Grinyov can't speak, but he must speak in order to clear his name from Shvabrin's slanders. He cannot speak because he would compromise the captain's daughter, so she herself offers Empress Catherine an explanation on his behalf. Or a person must defend herself, but cannot, because she has taken a vow of silence—the resolution of the story depends on her ability to prolong her silence. And so we get one of the fairy tales of the Brothers Grimm, "The Six Swans," and the story of "The Seven Viziers." But there may be another way of resolving a work, and this resolution is brought about not by semantic, but by purely compositional means, whereby the compositional element ends up being equivalent to the function of the semantic element.

This kind of resolution may be found in Fet's poetry: after four stanzas in a particular meter with caesura (a complete pause in the middle of each line), the poem is resolved not plot-wise, but formally—the fifth stanza, although in the same meter, has no caesura, and this produces a sense of closure.

Perhaps what distinguishes poetry from prose is the geometricality of its devices, the fact that a whole series of arbitrary semantic solutions is replaced by a formal, geometric solution. There is a geometrization of devices, as it were. Thus, the Onegin stanza is resolved through the final rhymed couplet, which disrupts the previous rhyme scheme. Pushkin supports this semantically by altering the vocabulary in these last two lines and by giving them a somewhat parodic quality.

I am writing about extremely general things here because I want to point out the most general signs, especially in cinematography. I have heard more than once film professionals expressing the strange view that, as far as literature is concerned, poetry is closer to film than prose. A great many people think this way and a whole series of films strive toward a resolution, which, by distant analogy, may be called poetic. There is no doubt that Dziga Vertov's *A Sixth Part of the World* (1926) is based on a poetic principle, with a pronounced parallelism and a recurrence of images at the end of the film conceptualized differently and distantly resembling, therefore, the form of a triolet.

When we examine Pudovkin's film *The Mother* (1926), in which the director has taken great pains to create a rhythmic construction, we observe a gradual replacement of everyday life situations with purely formal moments. The parallelism of the nature scenes at the beginning prepares us for the acceleration of movements, the montage, and the departure from everyday life that intensifies toward the end. The characteristic ambiguity and indefinite refraction of the poetic image, the capacity for simultaneous conceptualization through different means are achieved by a quick change of frames that never manage to become real. The very device that resolves the film—the double exposure of the Kremlin walls moving at an angle—is a poetic device that uses the formal rather than semantic moment.

We are very young in the world of cinematography. We have barely begun to consider the subjects of our work, but we can already speak of the existence of two poles in cinematography, each of which will have its own laws.

Chaplin's *A Woman of Paris* is obviously a prosaic film based on semantic elements, on things that are brought to closure.

A Sixth Part of the World, despite being commissioned by the State Trading Agency (Gostorg), is a poem of pathos.

The Mother is a peculiar centaur, an altogether strange beast. The film starts out as a prosaic piece with persuasive intertitles that fit the frame rather badly and ends as purely formal poetry.

The recurring frames and images, and the transformation of images into symbols support my conviction in the poetic nature of this film.

I repeat—there is prosaic and poetic cinema, and this is the main division between the genres: they are distinguished from each other not by rhythm, or not by rhythm alone, but by the predominance of technical-formal moments over semantic moments, whereby the formal moments replace the semantic ones, resolving the composition. Plotless cinema is "poetic" cinema.

ERRORS AND INVENTIONS

The End of St. Petersburg (1927) by Vsevolod Pudovkin leaves a dual impression on me. A double taste sensation. This can be explained perhaps by the changes in the script.

The script was initially conceived by Natan Zarkhi in the following way: the revolution takes place without a parallel romance plotline. The romance in the old historical novel scheme was advanced by historical events, and (in even earlier plot schemes) the romance itself advanced the historical events. Zarkhi's script took another direction—the ordinary, banal romance doesn't take place due to the revolution and the war. The feeling of comradeship between the heroes, the power of history over them restructures their love affairs, and the duellists become friends, while the unfaithful wife and the lucky rival of the officer become the allies of the cheated husband. The irony of the script was not sufficiently appreciated. The plot scheme was taken seriously, without irony, as a bourgeois plotline, and they simplified the film to fit popular demand, making it more suitable for the anniversary of the October Revolution.

The film that is being screened now is artistically weaker and politically less significant than what was initially conceived by the scriptwriter and the director. We are left with a plotline unfolding the story of a worker's family. This line is not juxtaposed against another plotline—it is simply pasted against a historical montage.

But art often moves forward on account of unsolvable problems and errors. An error that has been properly noticed and carried through till the end turns out to be an invention.

The absence of a plot construction in Pudovkin's film accentuated the problems of montage, questions of poetic cinema and narrowing of the shot. By poetic I mean, provisionally, the sphere of creativity in which semantic elements tend to become purely compositional. Thus in a poetic line, the rhythmic impulse subjects itself to the intonation of utterance. In its development, the phonetic aspect of utterance is also rhythmicized, so to speak, and the semantic elements engage in complex interrelations subjected to the law of repetition.

The periods, pauses, and articulatory aspects of a work—all become purely compositional elements. It is extremely important to note that in art a concrete semantic action can often be replaced with its compositional surrogate (this is not a term). So, for example, the presence or absence of a caesura in the last line can substitute the semantic resolution in a lyric poem. A temporal transposition can substitute a mystery. And retardation can be carried out not only with the help of a counteracting intrigue, but also the interpolation of extrinsic, neutral material.

On the other end of the poetic range is the purely transrational poem, which can be compared to the schizoid type as being the most extreme type of all psychopathological states. But then, of course, the term "pathology" does not have the same meaning here as it does in ordinary life.

The semantic moments in Pudovkin's film are poeticized following the principles of a signifying poem. He shows a real factory, which later transforms into a poetic montage phrase. The monuments of St. Petersburg are at first real monuments of a given city, but then they turn into a montage phrase and signs, whereby the Bronze Horseman signifies triumph and in a cellular montage becomes equal to a strike on a drum. Cranes and monuments, fanfares and drums turn into signs, into words. Their appearance in several montage cells is not fully visible, but only recognizable.

Physically, there are too few of them to be visualized. They are not fully articulated in the same way that words are not fully articulated when actually spoken. They are cinematic hieroglyphs.

Sergei Eisenstein is very evocative in his oral speeches. His not fully expressed theory of attraction, which does not remind the audience of their emotions but provokes their emotions, is extremely important for cinematography.

I think that if we were to attach dynamometers to the seats in a cinema hall we would find that even in a non-attraction film the viewers perceive an emotion because they experience it, even if remotely, and the aesthetic experience in this case is probably linked to the suppression of corporeal imitation. Something similar happens to internal discourse when listening to a poem.

There is another aspect of Eisenstein's work that is very intriguing. It is his concept of the need to narrow the meaning of the cinematic shot, to make it monadic, decodable in only one way.

As an example, Eisenstein takes the verbal construction "a thin hand," where the adjective "thin" would have to be filmed as one shot and "hand" as another. This would eliminate the possibility of reading the shot as "a white hand."

Eisenstein applies this technique in *October* (1928). For example, the machine gun is shown in this way. When the device fails, things turn out very badly—the result is comparison and symbolism. But these kinds of errors are usually the cost of invention.

The plotted parts of Pudovkin's film or, rather, its plotted part has turned out lamely. It has no antipode in the script.

On the other hand, his attempt to work with the distilled shot has produced in the shots of everyday life an extraordinary economy of materials, for example, the worker's bare room. In this bare room, on the table stands a sole cup of steaming tea. Due to the isolation of details the elementary plot device (the cup thrown against the window) has an extremely powerful effect.

Excessive details in old realistic works gave them an illusory quality. A work was comprised of signs that were not really necessary for its composition. These details, against which Tolstoy's critic Konstantin Leontyev protested, were similar to the details that experienced liars introduce into their stories.

The shot is distilled in Pudovkin and even the steam rising from the cup has a precise meaning: it shows how long the owner of the house has been gone and reinforces our expectation.

In terms of acting, the director wasn't quite successful in realizing his intention. Vera Baranovskaya, who played so well in *Mother*, exaggerates her act here and she alone falls out of the plot scheme of the film.

It is a good film, and rather inventive on the whole, but maybe it would have been better to invent something else. The director had to mask the absence of a whole section of the construction by developing the political part of the film and by employing a montage of pathos. He succeeded in doing this and, along the way, he was able to show the significance of the monadic shot in staged film.

There are non-accidental inventions in the film, such as the imperial uniform dress coats filmed without the heads and the frock coats listening to the declarations. All this is part of the technique of drying out the shot, of squeezing the water out of it. But it's a pity they didn't trust the scriptwriter and the director to the end. The authors had a right to test their invention. When you do not understand someone, it does not necessarily mean that he is wrong. It may just be that you have fallen behind.

After viewing some extracts from Eisenstein's film, a man who is intelligent and well-versed in cinematography said to me: "This is very good. I like it a lot, but what will the masses say? What will the people we are working for say?"

What can you answer to that?

Were it not for the assignment of the time period, were it not for the revolution, Eisenstein and Pudovkin would be wild aesthetes now. And Meyerhold would not have experienced his second burst of youth, and would have produced *The Government Inspector* and *Woe from Wit* immediately after staging *Masquerade*.

Eisenstein is perhaps indebted to the time for many, if not all, of his achievements.

The new time demands its own cinematography. And just as instances of industrialization in cinema appear to be elements that are artistically progressive, so the political assignment now plays one of the most progressive roles in cinematography.

But we must not produce works to gain applause, to please immediately and to please everyone. We must give the audience time to mature to perception.

By the way, about the playwright Vladimir Kirshon.

Kirshon is upset by the fact that, like me, he is criticizing Sovkino's policy. And he points out the difference between us: "Shklovsky needs the revolution so there can be good films," says Kirshon, "I need films for the revolution." What a magnificent idea! Someone has already said this at the State Duma: "You need great shocks. We need a great Russia!"[59]

59   The statesman Pyotr Stolypin used this phrase to close an address on the land question to the second State Duma. This address delivered May 10, 1906, defended the government's land reform against calls for expropriation or nationalization. In his con-

But this is a most reactionary antithesis. It is based on a distrust of one's own cause.

The revolution is certainly beneficial for electrification, industrialization, cinematography. If it is not, if it is opposed to these things, it will be crushed.

You don't have to be jealous or avow that you love the revolution selflessly—it is the heir to our culture and the engine behind it.

Eisenstein was commissioned to make an anniversary film. He had already erred once and made *The Battleship Potyomkin* instead of the anniversary film *The Year 1905*. The fact is that a work of art cannot be developed on a theme. Because the word or the shot is not the shadow of an object, not the shadow of a cause, but the object itself.

Artistic construction demands thematic changes. If Mayakovsky's poem "Good!" is to some extent developed along a theme, it is only because the technique of poetic language is so high that the material can be deformed by the device itself.

The historiographical part of Eisenstein's *October* cannot be carried out fully. On the other hand, it is precisely this assignment, albeit erroneously realized, that has created a whole series of cinematic inventions in the film.

This is due to the ingeniously free treatment of the objects.

The revolution has taken under its care museums and palaces with which it doesn't know what to do. The first rational use of the Winter Palace was made by Eisenstein. He destroyed it.

October is constructed on the cinematic development of individual moments. Time is replaced with cinematic time. The doors open before Kerensky for as long as necessary. The bridge

---

cluding remarks, Stolypin stated: "The opponents of statehood would like to choose the path of radicalism, the path of liberation from Russia's historical path, liberation from cultural traditions. They need great shocks, we need a great Russia!"

goes up, or Kerensky ascends the staircase, accruing more titles, for as long as necessary, i.e. completely conventionally.

Cinema ceases to be photography. It already has its own language and the staircase of the Winter Palace signifies very precisely what Eisenstein wants it to signify.

The cinematographer faces the danger of dragging things out, which can be viewed as an error in technique. If, however this dragging out is itself overstretched, then other laws come into effect. And Eisenstein's film is entirely overstretched and based on its own laws, which require a new analysis. The semantic material of the film is languor. The Winter Palace languishes. The grimy women shock-workers languish amid beautiful objects. And the objects are shown in such an exaggerated way that by their sheer quantity they crush both the Provisional Government and themselves.

The Soviet languishes. A stone thrown up falls down. There are moments when it slows down and moments when it stops in midair.

Eisenstein has ingeniously overstretched the stop and this is probably historically accurate; the Civil War happens like that, because you can't depict it only through battle scenes.

Eisenstein's film is a cinematic event of great importance. For many it is a cinematic disaster. As it is known, the first train ran slower than the horse, and the camera work in Eisenstein's film is not ideal. Not everything is resolved within the shot, the relationship between the shots works better. It is very likely that the moment of invention occurred in the process of working on the film. Eisenstein was experimenting, and a reel of film, of course, is very expensive. We certainly do understand the significance of the regime of economy. And yet the most important thing is not to produce cheap films, but to create something valuable. And an Eisensteinian film, without the merit of its inventive

moment, its place in world cinematography, its moral significance as the triumph of Russian cinematography, even without
these things—has its own value.

This type of film cannot be compared to newsreels.

It doesn't get in the way of newsreels, and the newsreels don't
get in its way. These are different devices of creativity.

ABOUT THE BIRTH AND LIFE
OF THE FACTORY OF THE
ECCENTRIC ACTOR (FEKS)

This was a time when the frozen echelons drank locomotives on the road, like samovars.

When people played *gorodki* in front of the Hermitage.

When they bathed in the pond of the Summer Garden and herded rabbits by the Alexandrian Column on Uritsky Square. It was a time when Petersburg fluttered like a pennant in the wind, "between reminiscence and hope—the memory of the future."[60]

The pennant was red.

The factory chimneys weren't smoking. The frozen rollers jumped over the plates in the printing houses.

The sky was blue.

The air was thinned out by the revolution. The whole city was sailing under the October pennant.

The revolution was even filling the sails of those who didn't understand it.

The fences were burned. The streets had lost their houses, they were moving like a herd. Leaving behind the frozen pipes, they were probably going to the Neva to drink water.

---

60   From Vladislav Khodasevich's poem "Dom" [The House] (1919).

The Prospect of October Twenty-fifth is empty. A musician is playing something for the Kazan Cathedral on the clarinet in front of the House of the Book.

Zhizn Iskusstva and a FEKS poster in four languages are frozen-glued to the wall.

This was a time when the father and the grandson of the youth—Vsevolod Meyerhold—was about to arrive from the South.

It was a time when Blok spoke about King Lear at the Bolshoi Theater, while the Futurists glued their posters in the city squares.

The People's Comedy Theater, founded by Sergei Radlov, was based in the People's House then.

Their performances introduced a strong dose of circus acts. Not long before this or at the same time Yuri Annenkov staged Tolstoy's play *The First Distiller*. Petersburg (not yet Leningrad) hung suspended between the present and the future, weightless, as a cannonball between the earth and the moon.

This provided an impetus for experimentation.

There was also a very strong literary tradition in Petersburg.

Many writers walked as ready-made monuments. The experiment was directed against tradition. The selection of *The First Distiller* and its adaptation into a circus show was a provocation. The demand for a change of tradition was rooted in the exhaustion of the old tradition and its habitual ties with the old system of thought.

Before writing "The Twelve" Aleksandr Blok was "learning from the coupletists." The People's Comedy saw him often.

Maksim Gorky wrote, I think, a play for the People's Comedy called *The Hardworking Slovotyokov*, which was not published during his lifetime, but it was staged.

The first who responded to the FEKS announcement written in Russian, German, French, and English were the coupletist, "actor of the ragged genre," later circus-man Serge and the Japanese juggler Tokoshima.

The first production of the FEKS was Gogol's *Marriage*. This *Marriage* of 1922 is connected with Eisenstein's and Sergei Tretyakov's *Wiseman* (against Ostrovsky) and stands against Meyerhold's 1926 production of *The Government Inspector*, which supposedly was a reworking of the classic play. The FEKS and Eisenstein tore down the classic, while Meyerhold reconstructed it. Nikolai Forreger staged in Moscow an eccentric play based on Mayakovsky's poem "Being Good to Horses" at the same time or almost at the same time with *Marriage* (produced by Kozintsev and Trauberg).

The production artists were Eisenstein and Yutkevich.

It is difficult to trace now why exactly Eccentrism, through Eisenstein, the FEKS, and partly Meyerhold, created the new devices of post-October art.

It is possible that Eccentrism emphasized the shift of interest toward material and construction. In any case, the theory of the montage of attractions (of signifying moments) is linked to the theory of Eccentrism. Eccentrism is founded on the selection of impressive moments and on a new, non-automatic connection between them. Eccentrism is a fight against the habitualness of life, a rejection of its traditional perception and presentation.

It is interesting that those who passed through Eccentrism were especially able to master the new material. Eccentrism, not as a method of presenting the material, but as a distinct realm of the material, is but a historical phenomenon now.

It was vital in the same way as the obsession with drawing columns during the epoch when the laws of perspective were being working out.

With the conventional *Devil's Wheel* and *The Overcoat*, with the contemporary *Little Brother*, the FEKS destroyed the rearguard of the enemy and came to *S.V.D.*—the most decorated film of the Soviet Union.[61]

The film can be praised for mastering the new material. The author of the script, Yuri Tynjanov, showed in his novels *Kyukhlya* and *The Death of the Vazir-Mukhtar* that the new method can dethrone old art from its primordial position. *S.V.D.* is certainly one of the best Soviet historical films.

It is done remarkably well, but in the future the FEKS directors would like to work on contemporary material or material that is historically contemporary. Now they are seeking approval for a film on the Jewish agricultural colonies or the Paris Commune.

Because as Gotthold Ephraim Lessing wrote in his *Hamburg Dramaturgy*, not everything that can be done remarkably well is worth doing.

People get offended, saying that film factories do not read scripts carefully.

I get offended, too. They read my scripts carefully, but they change my words.

The average member of the Artistic Committee cannot not change a script.

A script divided into shots probably appears rather defenseless.

But on the other hand (as they say in newspapers)—what are they *really* submitting?

Once they brought in a script for *The Government Inspector*. Pudovkin was sitting in the room with me. I asked him without looking at the script:

"How should an unsolicited script for *The Government Inspector* begin?"

"A pig is rubbing up against a post," Pudovkin replied.

---

61   *Soyuz velikogo dela*, also known as *S.V.D.* [*The Union of the Great Cause*], directed by Grigori Kozintsev and Leonid Trauberg, 1927.

I opened the script and read: "1) Close-up. A pig is rubbing up against a post."

SERGEI EISENSTEIN AND "UNSTAGED" FILM

The question of so-called "unstaged" film is very complex.[62]

In the infancy of Soviet cinematography people insisted that unstaged film was life caught unawares.

In reality, however, it turned out that "unstaged" film is primarily "montaged" film. And montage pieces require a setup or stopping for the shooting.

In one of Vertov's *Kino-Pravda* (*Cinema-Truth*) newsreels devoted to the radio, I saw one of Vertov's assistants playing a peasant. And according to *Pravda*, he was a middle peasant.

Even if we were to "catch life unawares," the very fact of "catching" would nevertheless be artistically directed.

---

62   The term "unstaged film" refers to the approach in early Soviet cinematography, particularly Vertov's, of using factual material and non-actors to depict the real world or, in Vertov's words, "life caught unawares," as opposed to "staged film," which included scripts, sets, props and actors. Vertov wrote in his manifesto "The Factory of Facts" published in *Pravda* (24 July, 1926), "Not a FEKS, nor Eisenstein's 'factory of attractions', not a factory of kisses and doves (film directors of that ilk have not yet become extinct), nor a factory of 'death' either (*The Minaret of Death*, *The Bay of Death*, *Tragedy in Tripolye*, etc.). Simply: A FACTORY OF FACTS … Flashes of facts! Masses of facts. Hurricanes of facts. And individual little facts. Against cinema sorcery. Against cinema mystification. For the genuine cinefication of the workers' and peasants' USSR" (In *The Film Factory: Russian and Soviet Cinema in Documents 1896-1939*, Richard Taylor and Ian Christie, eds., London: Routledge, 1988).

In the works of Stendhal, Dostoevsky, we find inclusions of unstaged material, but these are nevertheless aesthetic works. Therefore, the rejection of staging or the inclusion of raw material is neither a necessary nor a sufficient basis for judging a work to be unstaged or non-aesthetic.

Moreover, we may say boldly that it is precisely in newsreels that we come across staged material. I know that some moments of the February Revolution, such as the passage of the armored cars, were staged because I myself watched the enactment. I have seen some shots of Lev Nikolaevich Tolstoy and it seems to me that even this self-confident man was playing to the camera a little. It is very difficult to teach someone to walk in front of a camera as if he hasn't noticed it.

There are only two solutions to this: either every single person must be taught film acting, but that would be as ridiculous as driving a wall into a nail. Or we must select people with professional skills, which would be suitable and standardized to a point where they would not change during filming. But if we are going to choose a selected seed to sow, if in the villages we are now introducing pedigree breeding stock and castrating all non-pedigree bulls and stallions and not letting them, in Tretyakov's words, cultivate a sexual aesthetic, why shouldn't we have a selected person for the screen who ideally should be an actor?

The film actor is usually the biological and social ideal of his audience, and replacing the actor with a passer-by would mean retreating from industrialization.

I am not rejecting the grandiose work done by Dziga Vertov. I am only rejecting the parts where he uses large intertitles. It is not the work with random models that proved productive for the selection of cinematic form in Vertov, but the transfer of compositional problems from the sphere of plots to the sphere of pure juxtaposition of facts.

At the moment Sergei Eisenstein is not working with unstaged film, but he is working with plotless film. There is an old saying that "the dead seize the living." The saying has become a petty-bourgeois idyll, because now the dead don't seize the living, but ride them like a tramcar.

Someone once invented the method of joining semantic pieces through the fate of a single hero. But this is not the only method and, in any case, it is a method and not a norm. This method, this technique can work in some cases, but not others.

The easiest of all is to apply it to the story of how a man meets a woman. And this is why so many plotted works end with a wedding.

But now is not a time for domestic affairs.

And yet, the dead ride the living.

I was recently commissioned to rewrite worker-correspondent (*rabkor*) themes, to write a libretto. It was about a man and a woman. The woman was expelled from the Komsomol cell. When I had written the libretto I gave it to the worker-correspondents of the newspaper to read. One of them made a suggestion: "Shouldn't the secretary of the Komsomol cell also be the woman's husband?" The director asked: "Could it really happen that a husband would expel his wife or admit her without anyone objecting?" No, they said, it could not happen. But people are used to thinking in terms of kinship.

Eisenstein says that if today a scriptwriter is commissioned to show war from seven different perspectives he must invent a family with seven brothers.

In the meantime, the technique of art shows us that compositional devices can replace semantic ones and produce the same effect. Even in literature, for instance, we can resolve the composition of a novella by introducing a parallelism. Or we can create a plotted mystery with the help of "lost documents" or simply by rearranging chapters.

Cinematography today is not in need of traditional plots. Eisenstein's *The General Line*, *The Battleship Potyomkin* (let it get used to second place), *October* are films that are not held together by kinship, they are staged films, but they are material-oriented and plotless. And the latter two qualities of this division are far more important than the very conjectural former quality. The task of unstaged film has turned out to be useful in a subsidiary way, as the impediment that created a new technique for resolving the problem. But plotted cinematography (i.e. commercial scriptwriting) exists now only as a mummy.

Unfortunately mummies are everlasting.

RALLIES AND TAKEOFFS

COUNTRY ROAD

I had fallen behind the car rally in Moscow. I had to let the editorial staff of *Ogonyok* know about this.

"You can reach the cars by airplane," they told me.

I am a compliant person, and someone else's decision sucks me in like a ventilator sucks in a fly. A car came to pick me up in the morning. We were already at the aerodrome by seven o'clock. A Junkers was taking off right then for Königsberg; it was strictly on schedule. I wanted to sleep, and not be fascinated by planes. A big Dornier was flying to Kharkov; its wings were above the cabin and attached to the body of the plane by a connecting rod on each side. You can't see the rods on the Junkers, they are tucked inside the wings. On the other hand, the Dornier can carry eight people. It has eight woven chairs in the cabin, and you can enter the stokehole from the cabin. Everything is rather spacious. The baggage section is at the end of the cabin.

There were only three of us flying. They gave us pink, waxed cotton balls in an envelope with instructions and advertisement on it. Everything in Germany is in envelopes with advertisement and patent included. The balls were obviously German. We had to plug our ears.

The machine rolled by the joyful, slim-boned, muscular bomber destroyers at the far end of the field and like a silver crow started its takeoff run. The wheels thundered over the rough ground, the dry red grass of the airfield. We rose into the air from the other end of the field. And, as always, we didn't feel how the plane lifted off the ground.

The morning Moscow hangs below us. A familiar circle over the aerodrome. We are flying to Kharkov. Below stretch the harvested fields. And you see from the airplane not what is large-scale, but what is numerous. You get a general view. Now you can see stripes left after reaping. The ground is marked by semicircular parallel lines. It looks like a row of planks seen from the ends. There is something else lying in the fields. They probably reaped, but did not gather. What do herds of cattle look like from an airplane? At first I thought ripped pieces of paper. But no, that's not right. They look like handfuls of small red and black skulls, strewn across the fields. We are in midair. There are trees below. Haystacks by houses and threshing floors with scattered yellow hay. You can see a lot of bread from up here.

But the flight to Kharkov is only four hours and apparently I slept through three. As a consolation, let me tell you about an incident involving Andersen, the fairy tale writer. They had just invented the railroad. Andersen got on a train. He was probably amazed then that the train to Königsberg left on time and he kept trying to mark down the time of departure. Then it passed through Germany. "We are entering the Grand Duchy of Darmstadt," said the man sitting next to Andersen, offering him his snuffbox. Andersen took a pinch of snuff and sneezed. "And how long until we pass the Duchy?" he asked. "We just passed it while you were sneezing," his neighbor replied. Since we were just celebrating the centenary of the railroad, please accept this anecdote (you can find it in the collection of Andersen's works) instead of a description of my flight to Kharkov.

My neighbor woke me up: "We are descending." Kharkov was already below us, vast, verdant, lavishly interspersed with the bright red color of the newly rising buildings. We are descending. Now we are rolling into the aerodrome. There is a huge hangar that houses gray doves—the Dorniers. It has a high ceiling, like that of a terminal. There is a sign in the corner that says: "Head of the Station." And no cafeteria in sight.

"Did the car column leave already?"

"Two hours ago."

I threw my suitcase on the ground out of disappointment. But fueled with hope that the Russian potholes might snatch two or three cars from the tail of any car column, I went to the starting gate. The jagged tire tracks were still fresh on the dry highway.

"How long ago did they leave?"

"The Agea left ten minutes ago."

So, the car from the fourth column that had fallen behind was already gone. But suddenly I hear a humming and then the Packard appears. I recognize it by its radiator. It is an eight-cylinder car from the first column. I raise my hands like a derelict and ask to be picked up. They stop for me. It turns out they were delayed because they had to repair the springs. One more car is being repaired in Kharkov. We drive. The road is wide. It stretches along a row of telegraph poles. It is frayed and ragged like woolen yarn. From here on there is no road, only a direction. Each driver must find his own way.

It didn't rain yesterday. The road is tolerable. There are harvested fields on both sides of the road.

We are following the tracks left by the other cars along the soft steppe road. At some point it seems that we are lost, but the corpse of a big black dog with white spots gladdens us. It means that our cars have passed through here. The road to Chuhuiv turns to mud. It is liquid black soil. The strong Packard with its wide balloon tires drives right through it. The smaller cars are stuck in the mud up to their radiators, pushing it forward with their muzzles. We pass them. We are passing the Adler 30. The car and the drivers are all covered in mud. They barely have the strength to greet us. We drive on. Chuhuiv. The whole town consists of identical three-window houses with columns and frontispieces. The roofs are tile. This used to be a military settlement. Here the Russian double-headed eagle tried to transform into a Roman eagle. Arakcheev's decorative brick fences stretch off into the distance.

In the town we are greeted by an entire military division planted in espalier-formation and residents who shower us with flowers and parcels of nuts. Then we pass by the camp on the left and appear in the steppe again. We catch up with our column by the outskirts of Izyum. They were dining there. We don't stop, of course. We drive on.

The road goes uphill. Chimneys on the horizon. I count them—there are thirty. We drive into a town. It's Slavyansk. The road winds through factories. It smells of chemistry, dust, and industry. We are greeted by thick espaliers of people. Rows of children, yellow from the sun, gray from the dust. There are hundreds and thousands of them. They greet us with friendly applause. We are showered with flowers again. There are notes in the flowers—greetings from women and their addresses, extensive messages from the organized artisans with statements about the significance of automobilism, short instructions such as "Don't drive over hens," and questions from young pioneers like "What do pioneers do in Moscow?" We laugh in the dust out of joy. People standing on the corner carefully throw melons into each car. They throw branches of plums. Then there are more children standing in only striped underpants and applauding. Slavyansk ends. The road is not too difficult after Slavyansk. We see the chimneys of Artyomovsk toward the evening. The cars line up around the huge concrete monument to Comrade Artyom in a pseudo-Cubist style. It's dark already, the greenery of the city looks dense. My comrades who knew that I had fallen behind in Moscow greet me. Everyone is running to the telegraph station. The *Pravda* correspondent A. Perovsky has already occupied one of the windows.

We have to pass the night in the dormitory of metalworkers. We pass by the town square again. The dusty Adler stands sullenly in the fourth column amid small cars like a failing student who has been retained in the same grade.

The morning dawns. We are having tea at Narpit.[63] The Germans are complaining that the cars are overloaded, while the drivers are arguing about outracing each other yesterday. Clärenore Stinnes is demonstratively washing her mini Ade. People go to look at the Renault Taxi. The poor little car. It was designed for city driving, with only one spring in the back and a comparatively heavy *coupé*. But it's still in good shape. It might even reach Tiflis. I don't want to ride in the Packard. I try my best and end up in another American car, the Pierce Arrow 27. It's a good car, but its top doesn't come down, which I had the chance of finding out only later.

The real road began from Artyomovsk.

At first everything was fine, and the cars were running, gathering speed in intermissions.

The road was all in dust. If seen from afar, the steppe looked like an artillery battlefield.

The smoke of individual cars sometimes merged completely when the column grew tighter. Then it looked like a smoking comet. The hills were to the right. The road danced, trying to throw off the cars. Then we saw red hills with deep holes that

63 People's Nutrition, established in 1923 to oversee the feeding of the general population.

sloped to the side. We were being thrown up against the car's ceiling. The road would run straight down to the devil, then suddenly find a bridge or skip over it.

The last eight versts to Shterovka were terrible. But soon in the valley by the river we see a gray multistory building made of concrete. It is Shterovka. They have written "Welcome" on the gates in all languages. And everything is woven with oak leaves. Women workers greet us with applause as soon as we drive in through the gates. And right after the gates is a museum-caliber pothole: down, to the flanks, to the side! This pothole deserved a special sign. We find out that the elastic connector between the gearbox and the discs of the Lincoln has been torn. The Packard has broken springs. We are examining the edges of the fractures. It is a casting defect; they will have to show it to the car company.

We are served dinner on the upper floor of the station. But a minor incident gets in the way. We were supposed to stop in Shterovka for only a couple of hours. But the inertia of people's habits prevailed. Someone decided to survey us: What is the model of the car? How much horsepower does it have? Who is the owner? Who is the mechanic? Where was the car built?

The survey ruined our impression of Shterovka.

Shterovka itself is a half-finished power station for the electrification of Donbas. The first machines will start working this winter. For fuel, the station will be using what is called "culm"— the waste or slack from anthracite mining. Shterovka will provide electricity to an area within a radius of nine kilometers by burning this very culm. For now, it threatens the area with a black flood. There are already thirty-five million poods[64] of culm in the neighboring mines. Originally the station was designed to produce twenty thousand kilowatts of energy, but they also

64   An old Russian unit of weight equal to approximately 36 pounds.

foresaw the possibility of expanding its capacity to a hundred thousand kilowatts.

They built an embankment dam on the Mius River for cooling the turbines. The size of the reservoir is about fifty desyatins. The fuel will be fed mechanically into the fireboxes out of suspended bins from above.

The good food and cordiality of the workers helped us forget about the survey. The firefighters offered to wash the cars. That was very hospitable of them, but it was not really necessary. Then back on the incredible road again with almost no signs.

The slag road turns to clay again.

The road winds in zigzags.

We reach Rostov by three o'clock.

We are met by a crowd of people and the yellow tents of mineral water sellers.

I look through our column, almost all of the cars have deflected springs.

It was a tough road for all of them.

Now it is possible to say something about the results of the rally.

Two thousand versts have been covered.

The Mercedes, the Steyr, and the Sunbeam are all superb in speed.

In terms of fuel economy, the Fiat in the first column wins first place.

The Adler in the second column comes second.

And the Tatra in the fourth column takes third place.

Oil consumption is low in these modern cars: some cars drove without having to add any engine oil since the departure from Leningrad.

All in all, the results of the rally are significant. The cars will obviously prove that they can acclimatize to the USSR.

THE VILLAGE MISSES THE CITY

Recently I was supposed to fly on an airplane from Moscow to godforsaken Boguchar.

We flew out of Voronezh and flew along the Don, while often stopping in villages.

The villagers, as it turned out, would leave their fieldwork and wait for the airplane.

They run to the airplane as though we are handing out money. They sit by the plane for nights.

The villagers don't like the car, but they certainly like the airplane.

The village is not completely mundane. It has an interest in what is useless today. The villagers like to generalize all the questions. They move from the particular to the general.

And the airplane is interesting to the village, mainly the old men, as a spy in the sky.

"Is there really nothing behind the *khmara* (clouds)?"

Very naïve.

In the meantime, the engine is not news to the village.

They know it and appreciate it.

The peasant doesn't want to be an engine himself.

It is boring for the peasant in the village today. He wants to turn the village into a city. He says: "The ox works for the peasant, and the peasant works for the ox." This circle is not very popular in the village.

The village likes sensations, numbers, inventions (and they must be Russian), electricity.

I think that the illustrated journal would work very well in the village. Only it can't be populist and has to be without any pretty pictures depicting haymaking. In our conversation with the peasants we have always called our Junkers a *samolyot*, while the peasants have always called it an *airplane*. Foreign words are popular in some parts of the village. They call chalk *Kreide* in all of the Voronezh province. The village needs a newspaper full of events, city techniques, and it will figure out the rest on its own.

And the village apparently doesn't need peasantrified literature.

It is useless in the form that it appears today (imitation of popular speech) for writers, too.

I have had the chance to see a writer's manuscript at the Ivan Nikitin Museum, which had been corrected by Lev Tolstoy for his publishing house, The Intermediary.

Tolstoy had crossed out, first of all, words such as "azh," "agromadny" and other verbal garbage that imitates popular speech.

Popular speech can be used artistically, but of course all of Leskov's "popular etymologies" were created specifically for the people.

They were imported goods.

It would be great to photograph and publish the manuscript with the Tolstoyan truth.

Then they wouldn't say that Lidia Seifullina goes from Tolstoy to Tolstoy (as tramcar A goes from Gogol to Gogol).

There is not a lot of old culture in the Voronezh province apart from the manuscript with Tolstoy's corrections.

Life there is starting only now, or it should be starting soon.

The old culture didn't leave anything behind.

The newspaper will be virtually the first piece of literature in the village.

The newspaper must help the village become a city.

Left on its own, the village is now doomed to a life of cheap, non-renewable engines.

The sand blows right through it.

The sun dries it.

The gopher is not a very large animal, but even he can eat up an entire village.

ON THE AIRPLANE

It is difficult to describe a flight, as it has been described so many times.

General impression: the ascent is pleasant, the descent is unpleasant, turbulence is worst of all, and when the plane is turning, when one wing is higher than the other, you want to grab onto your neighbor.

The machine that's carrying me is a Junkers. It is made of corrugated aluminum. None of the braces are visible, they are inside the fat metallic double wings. The gasoline tanks are hidden in the wings by the passenger's cabin. It has a hundred and eighty horsepower, six-cylinder engine, dual controls—both the pilot and the motorist, who sits next to him, have the same levers and pedals. The plane looks like a bluntnose fish if we discount the wings. The pilot and motorist get in and out of the fish eyes. There is a small cabin for four passengers. The interior recalls that of a loge in a German theater, i.e. upholstered with some patterned material and furnished with pom-pom curtains.

From the windows of the cabin you can see the sturdy wings that fly next to the plane like two boxcar roofs. Below, say a verst lower, you can see the provinces passing one after another.

Everything is so generalized below that it seems new. You can see herds of cattle. Little squares—peasant houses, with black squares inside—their yards. Fields laid out tightly next to each other and crisscrossed in different directions.

It is turbulent (there is a strong wind). The worst turbulence was when flying over Ryazan. The fields keep getting bigger. A field looks blacker through steam.

There are more ponds than streams.

We parked in a field right under Voronezh, then flew over to the Voronezh River.

The Voronezh is a narrow river that fills with water only in springtime. Taking off was difficult, because we kept pushing against sandbanks.

The Junkers is a heavy machine. It needs to pick up speed before it can take off, whereas the Voronezh is not only narrow, but also curved, and even has a small bridge.

Now the plane is parked on the Don and it is content.

We took it through the counties.

Bolshak.

You can come here either by plane or on a pair of oxen.

The watersheds are located in the high desert.

The peasants go out into the field for a week. They bring water in barrels and sleep by the carts.

Landowners have been driven out, but it is more important to drive out the gullies from the fields.

The field is infected with gullies as if with syphilis.

Landslides because of water and winds.

People need to organize themselves. The pulverized peasantry can't do it alone. The city must merge with the village—that's the only way to save the culture.

There was no harvest and will be no harvest here. The rains are always ill-timed.

The quantity of precipitation is just barely enough, but water does not arrive when needed most and disappears into the dry, gullied soil.

The ground is riddled with holes.

One ought to stay in a steppe for a few hours without water and see people, who have not washed for a week, slaving away in their fields in order to understand what has been achieved.

People are saving disappearing rivers. The Silent Pine River has been dug out and recovered. They dug it out, increased its velocity, and now it will carry water from two thousand and five hundred desyatins of land. All in all, they plan to drain six thousand desyatins. The working conditions are harsh. Malaria is defending its hereditary realms. People have been working in water up to their chest. Now they have new pumps and they are pumping out the water.

The local population observes the river basin management works with some strained interest and the Silent Pine River has given work to twenty-four thousand people, who toil in the cold water every day.

Lands rescued from the swamps will be handed over, of course, to the local population.

Everything around is very poor. There is no culture here whatsoever.

But it will come with water and it will change the ruthless, impenetrable need, which this land has known since Mammoth Age till yesterday.

WHAT'S BEHIND THE *KHMARA?*

Khmara means clouds.

"What's behind the *khmara?*" ask the peasants into whose villages we arrive.

By "we" I mean the "Face to the Village" agit-plane. It flies through Voronezh, Liski, Boguchar, Astrakhan, Guryev, and other cities to Moscow. But it does not pass over villages—it flies into villages and takes the peasants on a flight.

I have already written that there is very little water here—it can only quench the malaria mosquito.

This is why there are huge villages by the Don and by any other disappearing river.

You can pass through such a village on horse in one hour. It can also burn to the ground in one hour.

The population in Mamon village, where we are staying, is fifteen thousand. The plane in the air, in a good pilot's hands, is a wonderful means of communication. But as any nimble flying bird, the plane has weak legs and can break during touchdown.

Ours is a hydroplane. It has big black floats instead of wheels, each weighing twelve poods. The plane takes off like a goose, running and jumping on water.

The pilot keeps pulling the yoke toward himself, then pushing it forward, while working with the depth controls. The machine hums, the water behind the plane turns into dust and foam. The plane stands on its end and slices the water even deeper.

You can never notice the moment of takeoff from the cabin. We don't fly too high.

There are dark rain clouds on our right. We navigate around them. The land, seen from the plane, does not resemble rural land—it seems characterless and geographically generalized.

What you are seeing is not everyday life, but a quote from geographic and politico-economic data. You are seeing strips of farmland, and they resemble a row of green paintings of varying textures.

Now the intermingled strips turn into perfect, large, solidly colored squares, which means that they have switched to land-use planning, and bread is ripening in the fields.

Apart from regular perspective, Italian painting also employed an equestrian perspective and a frog's perspective.

In the future, painting will employ a pilot's perspective. Then we will describe it.

It is difficult for a pilot to descend into calm water: it is hard to calculate the distance from the water. Your own reflection is flying right at you from the depths of the water. But our pilot Moiseev landed the plane with a smooth touchdown on the water. His "bird's instinct" also had a "goose faculty."

People are already waiting on the riverbank. They had been waiting for several days. They were getting disappointed, even started to deride their Aviakhim,[65] but kept waiting.

We arrive early in the morning. Those who had been sleeping run to us from their huts. They wash by the river. A meeting is convened.

65   A society called the Friends of the Aviation and Chemical Industries, which was founded in 1925 to raise chemical consciousness, to generate public support for state policies, and to promote aviation through the orchestration of aeronautical spectacles, air shows, and agit-flights.

Then, after the meeting, we begin flying the peasants. The first ones to fly are the old men and women.

They ask to be flown higher. They want to know "what's behind the *khmara*."

The peasants like everything in the airplane, including the soft seats.

The young men climb into the airplane with confidence. The young women are afraid and ask that we fly them in pairs. The village does not like the car. It treats the car with enmity or indifference. But the village likes the airplane. We have flown over lands where there is almost no bread before the new crop ripens, but we have never heard anyone complaining that the airplane is a luxury. The seventy-seven-year-old woman, who was just up in the air, says to the others: "There is nothing in the sky, behind the *khmara*—it's empty." And then a conversation ensues by the airplane: "How much does an airplane cost?" "How much does it weigh?" "Will everyone be able to fly soon?" "How much will the ticket cost?" "Why doesn't the airplane fall down?" "Can my son become a motorist?" "If there is no God, why didn't it snow last year?" It is as if we are "eyewitnesses." When I tried to explain to a furious old man with white hair (he was shouting at me: "Don't interrupt!—You'll have your turn!"), he listened to me and said: "Why didn't you explain that earlier, instead of scolding me?" (it was his Komsomol grandson who scolded him).

There were some women sitting next to the old man. They disagreed with me. But they were gentle—they too were flattered by the fact that a person could fly.

Many peasants who have health problems are sent to Livadia now. That's very good, of course. But a healthy peasant is already sick of nature. He needs cars, airplanes, tractors, and electricillumination. The harvest is going to be good if the "*khmara*" don't get in the way.

THE VILLAGE IN 1925

SOME ASPECTS OF THE KRASNOKHOLMSK FLAX MARKET

The road to provincial, narrow-gauge Russia lies through Savyolovskaya Station. The train covers a distance of two hundred and thirty versts in seventeen hours. It stands in stations not knowing how to kill time. The train cars carry seasonal workers returning from Moscow and merchants going to the fair. The train is very slow. The versts crawl by. There is no town by Krasny Kholm Station; there is only a dirty circle around a park and several horse-drawn carts. The town is two versts away. Krasny Kholm is a town around two cathedrals. It is packed with people on a market day. Everything is quiet and empty on a regular day. The two-story building across from one of the cathedrals houses the local Proizvodsoyuz.[66] It is very lively here.

Everyone is leaving.

Tomorrow they are going to have their chief battle—the annual fair on Sergius Day in the village of Malakhovo thirty versts away. The money was supposed to arrive with the train, but it didn't. They borrowed money from the town, they went to all the companies, they scraped every cashier's window, and

---

66 An association for the organization of artisans into cooperative artels.

now they are stuffing the suitcases with money. The flax graders are already sitting on the carts. There is no place for me, because the horse cannot carry extra weight on such a road. They found a small horse for me, a small cart, and a small peasant. I could barely fit on his cart with my suitcase, but thirty versts is not a lot, and so I rode off. "My mare is ticklish," the peasant said. "Her front hooves are not shod and she's afraid of the high-way." The hind legs were not shod either, and we didn't take the highway.

It rained for several days.

The highway rose like a mound between two long swamps. "Our horses are used to water," said my coachman. "We live by the river." And, indeed, the horse carried the cart through the dirt with great enthusiasm. The conversation from Krasny Kholm Station has been on the same subject—flax and clover. Clover brought flax into this area, as flax grows well on clover sod land, which in turn has brought in the cattle.

We left Krasny Kholm by three o'clock.

We moved at a very slow pace and I didn't know what to do with my time. We had to spend the night in a village eleven versts away from Khabotskoe. The hut was clean, the walls had been washed, and the cockroaches were not so repulsive. "We smoked the wallpaper," said the host, and this was another example of the shortage of goods in the village. The grandfather moaned and groaned in the next room; he was sleeping in a sitting position, leaning against a dirty chest (they said, he had been sleeping like this for ten years). The host tried to coax me slyly into stay-ing overnight and letting the horse rest. He told me that he was from Leningrad and worked as a master confectioner there. He explained how "satin pillows" and candies with rum were made.

There are many workers from the city in the village; they all dream about the city.

Someone knocked on the window at one o'clock in the night. They were calling the hostess to break flax. Flax breaking usually requires assistance and the barn must be heated up. Eight to ten women work in the barn and break flax until morning, until the beginning of their workday. It is as if this nighttime work does not count. They process half a pood of flax straw per person with self-made breaks.

They work as fast they can, condensing the labor, as they need the money soon.

By two o'clock they woke me up too.

We took off.

The rains had wrecked three mills, and we had to go around them. The horses weren't ticklish anymore because the road went from furrow to furrow. An autumn road that rolled through the fields. They stopped us by a bridge and charged money for crossing. It was a bridge made by peasants, but those who took money from us were random people who weren't lazy to be awake at that time. They took fifteen kopeks. By the next bridge they were asking for fifty kopeks, but we were able to cross without paying. On the way back their technique had been perfected—they had taken down the bridge, said it was broken and took money not for crossing, but for fixing it.

We stopped once more to spend the night; it was a blacksmith's house this time, almost under Malakhovo.

Our host's family was very big. They slept everywhere—on the floor, on the chairs, on the wooden couches. Here they processed flax in the barn using a flax break with wooden rollers. It produced ten poods of fiber in eight hours. There were many breaks like that in the village. They could be rented out from twenty-five to fifty kopeks. They also had horse-drawn breaks.

The peasants use them extensively and even transport them from village to village.

The blacksmith was bringing six poods of flax to the market.

People speculated that the price of flax would go up by New Year. So those who were selling their flax obviously needed the money sooner. My coachman wasn't bringing any flax to the market and said that there wouldn't be much flax anyway, as the cooperatives had already bought up everything from the peasants, preventing them from taking anything to the market.

It was getting lighter. The stars were disappearing into the sky that was gradually turning azure. There was a glow in the sky somewhere on the left, as if a distant village was on fire. The sun was rising behind us. The roads were filling up with people walking to the fair. There were carts with horses tied to them, and foals with fuzzy backs jumping nearby. The tails of the foals were curly and woven like buns.

Malakhovo began with the horse market.

The roads were blocked with carts and horses. The sellers ran around the crowd, holding their horses by the bridle and showing them to possible buyers. The roads were packed with so many carts that even the sidewalks of a city couldn't come close to being so packed with pedestrians. The long axles of the carts were getting entangled and hooked to each other.

It was light now and slightly warmer. The legs of the giant tripod-scales were already jutting out of the crowd. By seven o'clock in the morning I was drinking tea in the quarters of the local cooperative association. The mood here was lively and almost reaching combative hysteria. The representatives of Khlebprodukt, Gostorg, Lnotorg were just here and they were conferring about keeping the prices within the set limits. They would come to an agreement, but then they would not trust one another. The chief representative instructed: "Our task is the following, whether there is a market or not, we must keep the price of flax fixed, but if they are against the limit in the market, they will ruin everything for us. We won't give in and sell the flax to them. We won't break the limit first, but if they do, then we'll have to break it too." The gray-bearded flax graders were getting anxious (there are many old specialists in the flax business). And here, in the market, amid the crowd, they kept forgetting that they were not buying for themselves and kept getting angry at their conscience. The trading commenced, as though breaking loose from the chains. The scales stood side by side in a row like cannons on a battlefield. But these cannons were "hostile" to each other. As soon as a flax producer would put out his scales, his competitors would surround him from all sides. There were scales not only in the center of the market but also at its edges. It was a raid of scales. Sometimes a rumor would spread that they were selling flax somewhere on the side, and we didn't have our scales there. All in all, they said there were sixty-eight scales, out of which twelve were ours, the rest belonged to Lnotorg, Gostorg of Bezhetsk, Raisoyuz, and private merchants who were suspected of working for Gostorg. The great mess created by the carts wouldn't let the horses and people move freely in the market. People walked carrying the flax behind their backs in large bales. The merchants would snatch out a bundle of flax, hold it between their knees and comb the ends of the fibers with both hands: "How much?" The buyer would offer his price. "No, that's too low," the grader would respond and name his price. The bargaining lasted a few minutes only, perhaps even less—half a minute. The sellers rushed from scales to scales. The mood was like that of a stock market. At seven o'clock good flax cost around nine rubles, then after nine o'clock it went up to eleven rubles and sixty kopeks. People barely had time to write receipts and, in order to speed up, they wrote the price right on the seller—5.50; 6.50; 11.50. If the price was high, the seller, even after receiving the money, wouldn't wipe out the price and walked in the market as a newspaper or a bulletin. That's how it was apparently done—buying up the flax and ripping away the ends of the fibers from the sellers, the peasants, like feathers from birds in flight. But when buying like this, measuring labor productivity becomes a matter of luck. The price of the flax obviously depends not only on its quality but also on the mood of the neighbor's scales. The graders were telling me that, if you wanted, the flax could be of higher grade.

The race was not only for flax, but also for the lines around the scales, because the peasant likes to squeeze in wherever there is a line, and so the buyer was afraid of losing his line. They ran around the market, ushering people toward their scales.

The trading had been going on for an hour already. The hills of flax kept rising on the mats. The bundles were swiftly thrown on the scales. The peasants watched distrustfully how the arm moved. They argued about a quarter of a pound, making sure that the weights were not fraudulent. Sometimes they tried to mix five-ruble flax with ten-ruble flax and, of course, were caught in action. But it seemed there were no instances of outright cheating, for example, short-weighing, which is very easy to do in the atmosphere of flax madness.

The trade continued for another half an hour and then it quieted down by the scales. People were still standing in lines, but the crowd around the lines had thinned out. It was obvious who the winners were. Some merchants were still walking around with loads of flax on their backs and offering it for outlandish prices. The peasant searches and finds his union in the market and offers his flax. The determining factor is the payment plan. Everyone here is talking about payment plans. The peasant almost always feels cheated in the market, because knowing how to insist on a price is a special skill, which someone who has created a good product might not have. Tortured and exhausted in the market, the seller comes to a cooperative, because they don't play word games with him here. He is hopeful that they will offer the right price. The cooperator takes such people from the market with a scornful tolerance.

Apart from flax, people were also selling a few sheepskins, some butter and eggs. The horses were in bad shape. A four-month-old foal cost between fifteen and twenty rubles. But a foal from the factory cost seventy-five and even a hundred and fifty rubles. That's how much the village values pedigree.

Yes, and regarding agitation. I didn't see a single piece of printed matter, or any slogans or posters in entire Malakhovo, even though thousands of people had gathered here, spent the night and were bored after they were done with their trading and left the market. It just hadn't crossed anyone's mind. The peasant has the sufficient mentality of a minor proprietor. He is easily excited by the sixty-eight scales in the market with their sixty-eight different prices. Moreover, the market tries to penetrate into the village as well, destroying the cooperation. The cooperative associations set a date for turning in the flax. The carts with flax arrive. This flax is already designated, it belongs to the cooperative, but other procurers arrive as well and they set up their own scales.

When the crowds left the marketplace, I filled my galoshes with hay and walked through the sticky mud. It was interesting to see what the peasants were buying in the market. They were buying meat, bagels, painted carts, wheels, buckets, cast iron at twenty kopeks per pound, tire steel, and manufactured textile by weight. It was the first time I was seeing something like this. There were many stands and some had the following sign: "Textile scrap by weight." The fabric scraps are rather large: from one and a half to two arshins[67] per piece. I asked about the

67   An old Russian unit of length equal to 28 inches.

origins of the scraps. The scraps were strange. For example, there were many torn head cloths that were patched with a sewing machine. It turned out they were factory defects.

When the product is found to be defective in a factory, whether due to a skipped thread or a faulty pattern, they tear the cloth into pieces and sell them by weight. The scraps are bought up by traders, sorted by color, put together and sewn, and sold to the peasants. Apparently, all this is very reasonable, just like anything else, but it's wild to think that they tear the cloth in order to sew it back together again and then sell it to the peasant. Apparently it is possible to fight for the quality only when there is merchandise, not when there is none. And then, they ought not to destroy the merchandise, but lower the price. A pound of textile scrap cost very little when I first got to the market, but then the price rose from a ruble to a ruble and thirty kopeks. They sold threads too, but they had only two colors when I was there—white and yellow. They also sold beads. The private trader's assortment recalled a lottery. In cooperative stalls the assortment was better, but with many defects.

Few horses were sold in the market.

Then it snowed. The snow was gray and heavy. They quickly packed away the purchased flax, tying it tightly with cattail ropes onto the carts, forming huge tight pillows. The road was worsening right in front of our eyes. The price for transportation kept going up. I got into my small cart, which had become even smaller because of a huge barrel crammed into it, and left.

We rode up to Krasny Kholm.

Here the driver got homesick again, and his grandfather got homesick as well and told through sighs that the horse can't go any further. The family was celebrating—the government had decreased the tax on food production. I sat for a while. Then I went to the barn, watched how they were scutching flax. Flax is not so great this year; the fibers are too short, and I saw bundles with black spots in the market. And now there isn't much flax left—it's disappearing from the matting. They were persuading me to stay overnight in the village again. I pitied the horse with its ticklish legs and decided to walk to Khabotskoe. The cart driver felt bad for me, but he pitied his horse even more. He came to see me off. We walked along the furrows, across the wet fields, through the wet snow. I was covering my face with my wet suitcase. The snow was melting. Going around Khabotskoe, making a big circle, I reached the factory from the back. I went up: it was warm there. I decided to stay there overnight. They showed me the factory in the morning. The Khabotsky factory is not large at all and resembles a manufactory. Now they are installing the ventilation system, and the pipes are placed over each wall. There was no ventilation last year and there was so much dust that it was even hard to see one's own hands.

Flax fiber is unfortunate fiber—it is still waiting to be processed in the factory. Cotton fiber is worse in quality, yet it crowds out the flax and seems to have been born especially for the factory. And the flax machines at the Khabotsky factory look somehow unreal: the vibrating part of the machine is made of cast iron and, of course, it cracks. But the breakers are not so bad. The spinning machines, and especially the Kuhlmeister machines, perform rather well. However, the scutching wheels are the weak point of the factory. There are eighteen of them and they are arranged in two parallel rows. These are clearly not machines but simple devices. This is what the scutching wheels probably looked like during the reign of Ivan the Terrible. Their productive capacity is two times more than that of manual scutching, and yet the actual output is lower than the output from manual processing. The eighteen wheels together don't produce even twenty poods per day. Of course, they scutch much better than the scutching knife, but the fibers are shorter. They were telling me at the factory that the quality of the fiber has improved recently. This type of conversation should occur in a workshop, not in a factory. Here you need to get used to the machinery, find out its secret. This year the trusts have stored up fifteen thousand poods. They need to produce a hundred thousand poods. From the stored up batch, nearly half is of the best grade. The peasants speak of the quality of factory production with respect, noting that you can't refine flax like that manually. But they complain about the prices. And the issue is not only the price. The breaking and scutching of flax is a difficult job, but it is not risky and employs cheap women's hands that are not protected by any professional union. Retting is more risky. This year some of the flax, though not a huge amount, got under the snow. There have been worse years. Rain is also an enemy to flax fiber. The peasant would gladly offer up the flax to the factory for retting. The factory takes from the peasant already retted straw, which could have been processed in two days and sold for money. And the factory machines that process flax are not real. Several workers must stand by each machine shoving it like a cart on a bad road.

It is, of course, more advantageous to leave the flax break in the villages because it will improve production and save labor.

But they obviously need to invent a different kind of machine for scutching.

In addition to dressing the flax, the factory also offers work in grading the fiber.

Peasant grown flax always has several grades of flax in each bundle, and in all truth, the peasant is always losing, because they appraise the bundle based on the cheapest grade. We need to change the grading system, make it more specific. Generally speaking, it would be good to eliminate the virtuosity, agility of the hands and ingenuity of the eyes from the flax trade.

Now the Khabotsky factory has stopped its work; it is waiting for new machines and firewood furnaces. It will restart its operation in a few weeks. They started to dig a reservoir on the grounds last year, but due to the offered wages the peasants stopped working halfway through. The work on the reservoir has been halted, and the peasants haven't been paid. The peasants aren't insisting on being paid right away because they don't want to spoil their relations with the factory, but they won't work either. Besides, it is not clear whether it is right to dig a reservoir in that place: there is very little water nearby.

People are saying that they should have built a bigger factory than the one in Krasny Kholm.

In the afternoon, the horses dragged me and another person from the factory to Krasny Kholm along an incredible road with frozen puddles. A troika carrying one of the flax graders passed us on the road. He got sick during the inspection of flax. It must have been from anxiety and exhaustion. We were moving slowly and reached the town in two hours. The train station was a few minutes away. In the station, several state contractors in Romanov sheepskin coats were discussing the battle at the fair as loudly as they can talk only in Russia. They were discussing the prospects of cooperation. Two Germans in splendid fur coats sat in the corner; they were probably from the concession.

A high railcar stood on the empty tracks in front of the station. I approached the railcar and talked to the driver. The driver was a bit reserved due to the fact that he was driving a car without a steering wheel, which, of course, completely disqualifies the driver. The men in the fur coats were indeed the concessionaires of Mologoles. They came to inspect the sawmills and the place where a woodworking factory will be built. Endlessly long trains with planks turned yellow from the snow were parked on the rails.

A locomotive kept attaching to and detaching from a train.

The Germans were sitting in the cafeteria and asking about wildfowl. And they kept taking off and putting on their splendid fur coats. The traders in the Romanov sheepskin coats were worrying and discussing how much flax was sold at the market yesterday.

They sold up to five thousand poods of flax, I think, and half of that went to the cooperation.

KNITWEAR DISTRICTS AND FLAX FIELDS

1925–1927

I once happened to pass through Likhoslavl. It is a station between Moscow and Leningrad. These are bleak places with large swamps, clay soil fields, and stones in the fields. Low moraine hills. Poor surroundings. But the villages here are wealthy and there are many new constructions. The new huts stand next to the old ones; they are evidently on reserve—not residential yet. This area seems to be particularly wealthy to those who have seen the black soil strip. The country roads are old, but there are new bridges across the creeks that haven't darkened yet. The villages are separated from each other with four-board fences and the gates are securely attached to the fences with wooden hinges. Behind the fences grows rye as high as human height. Buckwheat blossoms like a thick swarm of white flies coming up from the soil. Rye and buckwheat cope well with weeds. But the thistles and cornflowers stick out brazenly amid the crops. They are especially oppressive to flax.

It is summer. The traffic flow is yet not from the village, but to the village: they are bringing threshers from the machine associations.

The oats are looking good; they are actually foreigners from Australia. Unfortunately, there is not enough seed material. Some villages want to switch to communal harvesting, but they can't do it until they receive depersonalized, clean, graded grain.

On the mowed fields of clover you can see the small, red, wooly pods left for seeding purposes. There is not enough clover for the sowing and this disrupts the crop rotation plans. In some parts the soil is left unsown. The seed brought from Perm turned out to be good, while clover imported from abroad didn't come out the second year. The need for clover seed is great. Its demand is constantly growing. There is very little meadow hay this year, but those farmers who have sown clover will be secure in terms of fodder.

"This potato field is already a city," I was told in Likhoslavl. The city is already two weeks old. The border separating the city from the village passes through the fields, seizing them. The Kustselsoyuz[68] has an office in the city and a storehouse in the village, which is right across the road. This intermingled strip system is not accidental. The city and the village are intermixed in the everyday life of the region. So, for example, the Borovichesky district is populated by artisans—knitwear workers mainly. The knitwear machines are operated by women. They usually work two shifts of eight hours each. The union charges each worker a ruble and twenty kopeks per month for machine rental. The majority of the workers are members of a cooperative. In some associations cooperative members make up sixty percent. There are three cooperative factories for the sake of diversity. But some several thousand knitwear workers work for private proprietors. The cooperatives are not strong enough to unite them. The capital of the union turns over only twice in a year, while the equipment is loaned for three months.

The knitwear workers maintain a semi-urban way of life: the huts have wallpaper and the conversations are also very urban.

68 An association of artisan and farmer cooperatives and credit unions in Likhoslavl.

"Don't judge by the appearance of this hut," a peasant told us. "The wallpaper hasn't been reinstalled here for three years. They had a disaster last year, two of the horses fell, and the family doesn't have enough adult workers."

The knitting machine didn't hurt the agricultural economy, but it put an end to the three-field system.

It all appears to be a peasant idyll in the sense of Gleb Uspensky. He was the first in Russia who started a conversation about electrification. But he believed that electricity would save the village from being absorbed into the city. Electricity can be brought into every house: there will be an engine in every household, and then the village will be able to work on a home-based loom and spinning wheel to counter factory production.

Gleb Uspensky dreamed not so much of the electrification of the village as of the conservation of the village with the help of electricity.

Electrification is rapidly spreading in the artisans' villages in the Tver province. Three stations provide electricity to seventeen villages in the Likhoslavl district. Kuzino village was electrified two years ago of its own accord, without asking for the city's permission. In the autumn they organize big agricultural expositions in this village. They have a special exposition center and a mast for raising a flag during expositions. There is a building with an electric thresher and clover huller in the village square. They have been practicing crop rotation for a while here, but the peasants have also started experimenting with root crop rotation. They had been trying it in the past too, but unsuccessfully, and now they are recalling their failed experiments, and I don't know if this is a lucky time, but the turnips have turned out a good crop. The village of Kuzino is fenced from the neighboring village that uses the three-crop rotation system. There aren't too many such backward villages left in the province. The majority of cultured

villages are located on *otrub* lands,[69] but there are communal
villages that have been excitedly using the eleven-crop system.
The village of the knitwear district is happy not so much for its
economy as for the fact that it is starting to become a city. Things
are not progressing as Uspensky had envisioned.

"This potato field is already a city." This is not just in
Likhoslavl, and it is not merely a joke.

They have begun to value the labor of the women working on
knitting machines. The machine creates respect for labor.

They cultivate flax in this district, and flax is a labor-intensive
culture: it is threshed, retted, scutched, heckled. It can be processed by hand, of course, if you don't want to spare the hands.
It turns homes into barns full of dust.

For two years now the Kustselsoyuz has been attempting to
build a factory for the primary processing of flax.

The construction of the factory has begun, and they are
already transporting the bricks.

The factory is on a hill, by a lake. There once used to be a
pheasant farm there. Then they wanted to turn it into a museum,
but it didn't work out because you can't have a museum out of
a pheasantry without pheasants. Now they are going to ret flax
here and create a whole industrial complex around flax: a flax
processing factory, an oil mill, a power station, which will operate with a furnace, and a repair shop. Artisanal milling and traditional flax processing are coming to an end.

---

69   Established under the Stolypin agrarian reform in Russia (1906-1917), *otrub* lands
were detached from communal allotment lands and designated as the private property of
individual peasants.

POSTSCRIPT, 1927. The factory has been built.

People argued about flax processing factories while they were building it. It seemed that such industrialization was premature when they still had cheap working hands.

But the success of these factories is being revealed now: flax culture is expanding in the districts where they are building such factories, and some new types of crops are appearing: collective, produced from depersonalized, clean grain.

These are not just strips of flax, but flax fields.

SIXTY DAYS WITHOUT WORK

So what if I have already written about cars? I am going to write about them again. Osinsky motivated me with his article in *Pravda*. He is right—you cannot live without a car on these big roads. The old and not completely broken down cars are so ingrained in the way of life of our expansive country that if one were to get rid of them, or if they broke down on their own, we would have to serve time in a village. We would develop blood stasis and wouldn't be able to move our fingers.

The old station in Kiev is still standing and dozens of cabmen are parked by it for days, because Kiev is one of those cities that was supposed to move to another place, but cannot.

Cities, like nails and hair, are alive only when they grow. Sometimes a city might even grow on a dead quarter, just as a watch can run on dead time. But a city can also be dispensable. There is only one building being built in Kiev and it is nearly finished. It is true that they are also building a film factory, though it is not a building, but a covered space for the Jupiters, and it is not connected to Kiev, but is built in people's apartments.

Kiev is known for the Dnieper and Khreshchatyk Street, and the goods in the stores are the same as the ones that are so difficult to find in Moscow, and there are many casinos with the rules of the game, insolent and detailed descriptions painted on the windows. But Kiev is not a city that's alive.

Cities move. Novorossiysk is climbing over to the other side of the cove toward the cement factories. Dead Kerch, a city where women sit by open windows on a pillow, is transforming into a factory construction site. Petersburg is sprawling to the edges, and turning into a city-bagel with a beautiful dead center, whereas Kiev is an administrative city.

I was picked up in Kiev by an incredible car with a boy, who sat on the wing and poured gasoline out of a bottle into the carburetor, a falling roof, which the chauffer was holding up with his hand, and the chauffer's wife, who was always riding with him, because there were no passengers anyway.

After the battered car that had only two working cylinders, I got on a decrepit steamboat. It was a small steamboat with two paddlewheels and cabins that were more like cells. The captain's deckhouse was not in the middle but on the paddlewheels, so the captain was riding the boat like a woman, in a sidesaddle. The steamboat was about fifty years old and shouldn't have been allowed to operate anymore, because it could get stuck under a bridge.

When the world was created, the Dnieper was cut by rapids into two parts and this is why steamboats can't live on it. And so the old wreck is breaking apart.

The Dnieper is so serpentine that you easily mistake the right shore for the left shore in the marshes. If there is a counter-wind, the rafts going to the Dnieprostroi Dam are stopped for weeks.

I met with Fyodor Gladkov. He is not thrilled with the steamboat and keeps getting angry. He eats dinner and gets angry after dinner. A discontented person. It is stifling in the cells. Two people in one cell—there's no air.

The steamboat docks right by the bank in the wharfs, because the piers have been burnt and there are no new outgrowths jutting out on the water.

The market is by the steamboat—right in the water. The women stand up to their knees in the river. In the evening, lanterns illuminating the fairway ignite in the bushes like cigarette butts. The posts dangle with their reflections on the water like ropes.

We reach Dniepropetrovsk (former Yekaterinoslav). It is a lively city with a great future. And here, in the hotel, they serve information about Nestor Makhno along with tea from a samovar: "He was shot right here," they say, "in the elevator, and the machine gun stood in the yard, while I ..."—and they go on with their recollections.

Nobody knows anything about rapids at the newspaper office. They say: "Ivirnitsky is a historian, he knows, but he's gone."

We take a boat to Lotsmanskaya Kamenka and find a loodsman right on the riverbank. He has a green painted chest on wheels from the eighteenth century, an icon made from aluminum foil, and paper garlands hanging from the ceiling in his house. The floor is strewn with grass.

It is just the two of us on the oak, which is not enough. An "oak" is a large boat—that's what they were called in the eleventh century.

There are illustrations of animal life by Alfred Brehm on the walls as decorations. Later in Tiflis, I saw drawings depicting different forms of leaves taken from a botany textbook on a wall in a tavern. I was curious to find out what the owner of the tavern took those for. I asked him: "What is this?" The tavern owner calmly answered: "A boulevard." The nickname of the owner of the house in Lotsmanskaya Kamenka was Goryachi, meaning hot, spirited, but his real name was Yefim. He took us on a boat with two oars. At first his son was oaring, then I took the oars from him. The right oar didn't resemble the left one in its weight or length. Oaring the boat was as awkward as walking on a tightrope with a samovar (there used to be such a special Russian circus act).

The rapids hiss like Primus stoves. There are thirteen of them and they are separated with weirs. The water splashes against them, leaping up, and they call these waves "thunderstorms." The small whirling rapids are called "bull-calves," and they actually do make a mooing sound. The rapids are crossed on rafts. The rafts are long, their oars are made of logs—three in the back and three in the front. Navigating a raft is a desperate task. After crossing a rapid, the raftsman must immediately turn and steer toward the channel of another rapid, and always watch the water level of the rapid's fairway. The rafts go in fleets. The lead raft has a cabin—it carries provisions and the owner. It used to be the last raft, but now it's at the front to motivate the others.

We passed the first few rapids through the canals. The canals are laid through the rapids across the left bank, while the old goat path passes along the right bank. The water by the canals swells and curves inward, resembling a highway, i.e. the middle is high, the sides are sloping downward. It flows into the narrow space between two rock-fill dams. The waves carry the boat vertically, standing it on its stern.

Each rapid has its own character and the last ones are the most lethal. There is one with an especially good name— "Superfluous." And the rock right before Kichkas is said to be even more dangerous.

After you pass the thirteen rapids there is a rock called "School." This is where they have crashed the most. "Insatiable" is extremely terrifying. It is as wide as one verst and as long as one verst and a quarter. You ride on it for one minute. The water in its canal rises up so quickly that it breaks away from the banks. It is not water anymore but something completely hard and it carries the boat vertically.

The water breaks here, and after passing over several weirs it simply flows down a cascade. It is a storm, but each wave is affixed once and for all in its place, i.e. it has been beating against the rocks like this for ages and depends only on the height of the water.

There are landslides as deep as one and a half sazhens.[70]

It is strange to see the curving river. It falls not only down but also to the side. In general, there is nothing here that resembles our notion of water. But the most disappointing thing is when, after having been terrified to death and deafened in a place called "Hellfire," you see a fisherman standing on a rock.

It turns out that there is a quiet stream by that rock, and fishermen go up there and throw in their fishing lines and find that it's worth the try.

It is rather disappointing. Imagine that you have reached hell on some extremely difficult assignment and found there a man who was sitting quietly and drying his underwear.

There used to be huge platforms along the banks of the river for viewing, now they are gone—they have been dismantled and stripped to the last brick, except for the columns.

The columns remain as memorials. Some columns stand in a straight line, others in a semicircle.

The scenery is very impressive. There are small mills on the sides of the rapids that function on one-millionth of a rapid's power. If we were to compare, and it is expected that we compare, the mills resemble a three-kopek whistle attached to the storm.

---

70   An old Russian unit of length equal to 7 feet.

In the intermissions between rapids Fyodor Gladkov explains to the boatman the advantages of collective farming. The advantages are indeed very significant.

We hold onto our seats when going over the rapids. Once the bottom of the boat even hit a rock.

The shore behind "Insatiable" is verdant, and there are verdant wild pear trees on the verdant, steep, rocky shore.

I passed the night in the Sovkhoz—the state farm, the crop rotation of which is linked to the future Dnieprostroi Dam, because in any case the fields are going to be flooded. When they point out the survey pegs showing the future level of the river, it feels strange (not a very artistic word, but it's suitable here), strange to think that the houses, the hills, the islands, and the forests will go under the water, and that there will be a lake here, two or more versts wide in some parts.

It is almost impossible to imagine what they are doing in Dnieprostroi. It goes beyond the limits of what can be described in three hundred or even a thousand lines.

At night we argue about the Ukrainian language. The father of the family speaks Russian, the children speak Ukrainian, while the father would have liked them to speak English, and the children refuse to speak Russian, saying that if one were to speak the language of national minorities then they would have to speak Yiddish too. And this family argument has been going on for some five years. There is a family in Tiflis, where the father is Georgian, the mother speaks only Russian, and the eight-year-old daughter speaks only Georgian, which is why the mother can't talk to her daughter without a translator and feels very offended.

There are two or three more rapids behind the state farm, then the Dnieper turns sharply and you can only see the Kichkas Bridge hanging suspended over the river. I don't know who designed this bridge—people usually don't sign under bridges—but what I know is that Makhno exploded the central part of this bridge.

The bridge was so sturdy that the abutments were left intact, though disconnected from one another, and this turned out to be very useful for throwing down different types of loads. Now this bridge will go under the water, or rather, it would have gone under the water, but they will haul it to another place.

There is another bridge under Tiflis that was built, as they assert, by Alexander Macedonian, and it's called the Mtskheta Bridge.[71] But this bridge too will be dismantled soon because it has been flooded with water from the Zemo-Avchaly Hydroelectric Power Station on the Kura (ZAGES). The world in which we live today is changing extremely fast. And the rapids, through which I passed—they are the thresholds of establishments that are being liquidated. They merge according to the old Soviet custom and become Dnieprostroi with a thirty-six-meter high waterfall.

After the Kichkas Bridge, the right and left banks of the Dnieper recede, the river widens and shoals emerge on both sides. There is a rock on the left bank with a three-legged gypsum lion standing on it—this is all that's left from the former resort of Aleksandrobad. And on the right bank you can see rocks jutting out of the sand and the German houses of Kichkas village between the rocks—all of this will be under water soon, as the future banks are already being leveled by diggers with their horses turning like a carousel, dumping and spreading the sand around.

Kichkas is overcrowded with carts going in one direction, people pulling the carts, and conversing people.

I wanted to say "headquarters"—"establishment" sounds more like the immediate rear of a massive army. It is—even

71   Also known as Pompey's bridge.

more so—comparable to the moment when Austria was occupying Russia, only here the Germans are leaving their houses contented, as their houses are being bought, and besides, they are taking the bricks and tiles with them into the mountains.

The sound of hammering is everywhere. Bare hands breaking stones. Soon there will be a million cubic meters of stones. The numbers here, generally speaking, are in the range of millions. The diggers walk around in wide-brimmed straw hats.

I was received very cordially at the headquarters—the construction management. They told me many things and asked: "Please don't write about any of this, but you can stay here, and we will provide you with a room—then you can write. But don't write about how we build, as they have already muddled everything up in their articles about us." And so I didn't.

Gladkov stayed in Kichkas. He will write a novel, but Kichkas itself, full of constructions, will not be described.

Let's assume that I stayed in Kichkas for three more months. I think that I would have been able to write about how it is being built, how they are constructing cofferdams and why it is difficult and how they are exploding, but this book is not a novel consisting of five or six printing sheets—it is not made for the market.

You can write a feuilleton about the real Dnieprostroi, or you can write a big novel called "Elektrostroi" about the unreal Dnieprostroi, which contradicts logic, as there is much more material on the real Dnieprostroi than the invented one.

The passage from Kichkas to Zaporozhye was much more terrifying than going through the rapids. It was a holiday, and as they don't sell wine or beer in Kichkas, everyone was going to Zaporozhye. The steamboat was overcrowded and tilted over to one side, while the captain's assistant kept calmly persuading the passengers: "Return to your seat and play dominoes, because the ship might flip over onto its side when you stand on the deck.

We did you a favor by giving you seats." The steamboat kept going, tilted on its side.

INSERT. There are three types of smoke in cement factories that are interesting: gray, black, and brown, produced apparently from two different combustion processes and from the power station.

The factories are surrounded by gray and yellow dams, stacked with wood planks for cement barrels. The stacks resemble slave cabins (an improper comparison, I admit, but if one is going to describe, for instance, the sun, then he has to compare it with something, even if the sun is a familiar object).

I am so tired of comparisons that next time when I have to describe the clouds, I will write: "And the previously described clouds floated above the cement factories, above Novorossiysk."

The Terek in the Daryal Gorge does not leap like a lioness with a shaggy mane on its back,[72] but comparisons are not supposed to be similar. If we were really to compare, the Terek resembles more of a slightly loosened hemp drive pulley that wobbles due to transmission wear. Or maybe the Terek resembles the process of making rope from hemp fibers. Or maybe it is like the Dnieper rapids, only much narrower, but with the same unmoving waves affixed to the rocks. That, down there, is Queen Tamar's castle. It is small and looks like a lemonade stand. Up higher, the Terek is shallow and slow-moving. If we placed a bathtub across the river, it would probably fill up in two minutes.

Here the Terek recalls Moscow rains, when the water flows down from Volkhonka Street to Mokhovaya Street, and when the asphalt gleams. These hairy asphalt streets, heavily trodden

72   A reference to Mikhail Lermontov's "Demon" (1829-41).

by human feet, are like the tracks of camels that wipe their hairy feet on the glued sands of the desert.

If we were not to count the mills that spin a thousand times faster than the current—they have wide wheels and they float on double boats—there are also the wineskin rafts that float down the Kura. People get on such rafts at the edge of the city with wine and food, *zurna* and *duduk* players, and float down the river to music on the spinning raft.

In the place where the Kura joins the Aragva, and right under the "Mtsyri" monastery,[73] there stands a raft now—gray and clean as a surgeon's table. The river widens and turns into a palm, and the fingers of that palm slide into the turbines of the ZAGES as into a glove. At night this place is lit with yellow and red lights. The red lights hang, reflecting on the grate that obstructs the watercourse of the new Kura.

The steam engine is irritable. The internal combustion engine, especially the four-stoke engine, is hysterical. The calmest of all sources of electric power is the hydro-technical system. It is blue-blooded.

As I mentioned already, the "Mtsyri" monastery stands above the ZAGES. The goats climb on its cornices. There is an old altar in the monastery. Monk Illarion, who is staying at his country house, is a favorite among the feuilleton and sketch writers, because it is much easier to describe the monk than the ZAGES, and besides—one has to describe something if one has climbed up to the "Mtsyri" monastery. From up here you can see the flooded Mtskheta bridge and old factories in the city, which is also flooded almost to its brim. This city is floating in the lake of the ZAGES like a ladle in a tub of water. The old monastery is huge and made of yellow and greenish stone. Its cupola is made of roughly hewn stone with simple ornaments. Inside the

73 A reference to Lermontov's "The Novice" (1839).

monastery, like in a case, hides a small church cast in stone. It is as big as an airplane box, standing vertically on its end. Inside are the tombs of Georgian kings and the descendants of the Bagrationi dynasty.

I like translations done by people who don't know the language well. A Georgian man told me how a certain king killed his enemy and buried him at the foot of his throne, or at the foot of his bed (I can't remember), in order to step on him with his "first" foot.

The monastery is surrounded by a typical Georgian wall made of rounded stones, stacked in a zigzag fashion. This method of arranging stones and bricks in a fir-tree pattern seems to be local.

The wall isn't too high; it has small towers and embrasures with two clasped palms, as it were, above the embrasures that served as sharp visors. This was very convenient for throwing different objects at the attacking enemy.

Meanwhile, the ZAGES appears to be calm and in no need of description. So far the reservoir is filled to one-third of its capacity. The second line hasn't been constructed yet, and there are iron bars jutting out of the dam—the armature to which they will attach a box. The second line of turbines and the third one have not been started yet.

Tiflis likes the ZAGES, and the Georgians who are not terribly thrilled about the present, soften, when talking about the ZAGES, which works quietly and without interruptions. Today they build power stations like they build factories by installing the pipes first in the buildings that have nothing else inside them. The power station will be surrounded soon with factories.

As of today, the ZAGES is not working at its full capacity—it only illuminates Tiflis and maybe heats up the electric irons and the building of the Georgian Film Studio (Goskinprom), which is among the largest consumers of electricity. I think it uses, or will be using, one-tenth of a turbine.

Funeral processions are strange in Tiflis. People carry a portrait of the deceased in the front—an enlarged photograph in a frame. The crowd follows the portrait, carrying an open coffin with the deceased in it. The deceased is dressed ceremonially in a traditional red karakul hat, even if it is extremely hot outside. The duduk players follow the procession and play a funeral tune, whereas I am used to seeing them play at the restaurants.

Though the songs that they sing at the restaurants are also sad, whereby two play on the duduk and the third beats the drum with curved sticks and sings, as the other two blow their duduks sadly with puffed up cheeks. The song says the following, as Tsutsupalo translated to me: "Life is like straw, and everything will pass. There are many flowers in this beautiful garden, but only the gardener may pick them. Were I the gardener ..."

They put aside their duduks in the morning and pick up their wide tin horns and play a song to the rising sun.

But now the musicians are playing something for the deceased, who lies in a sheepskin hat. His head is slightly tilted toward the shoulder. It is very hot.

In the Vere Gardens, beneath Tiflis, people drink wine in the gazebos. Here I was met by a most hospitable Georgian. Gigo, an old chorister, who was playing on a leather-bound guitar, put his guitar aside and, looking around at everyone through his dark glasses, which he wore to cover his blind eyes, said in Russian: "Allow me to say a couple of words: in the old days, a nobleman built for himself a ship and went on a far voyage. The sea wrecked the ship, but the nobleman was saved along with his servant by holding on to a log. They were carried by the water for twenty days and on the twentieth day the servant asked: 'Are there any other unfortunate men like us?' The nobleman replied: 'That's not right—we are not the most unfortunate men—we will either reach the shore or drown. But if a man has nothing to offer to his guest who happens to be his best friend—that man is truly unfortunate.'"

Our hosts were obviously not unfortunate that day.

The city of Kutais lies on the banks of the Rion, and the Rion is a very fast river. Only rafts travel on it, departing from a region called Racha.

The rafts are made of thick logs that are wider than an arm's reach and the ends of the logs have holes for ropes for tying the raft together. That's how we do it in Vetluga too. I know from the Russian experience that ten percent of the wood is lost due to these holes, because the ends of the logs get damaged. The rafts that arrive in Kutais are furry and damaged from hitting against the rocks. The softened logs probably look like buffalo. The buffalo are covered in bristly fur—sparse in the front and almost bare in the back. But they certainly don't look like poodles.

The Rion flows in such a way that people can swim only in one direction: they jump into the water and swim, say, for half a verst, and then they get out of the water and run back along the bank. In a word, the Rion is an irreversible river, just as electric power transmission is irreversible and as time is irreversible. And down below, some eight versts away from Kutais, by the Rion Hydroelectric Station, the river enters a huge valley that looks blue from the corn. Here it widens and reaches Poti like water filled to the brim in a cup; it even seems to be slightly convex, especially by the banks.

The river flows through the low city, full of humidity and sighing frogs. It is dark. Provincial people stand by the not yet closed shops all dressed in white. People are playing dominoes in the cafés. They are loading manganese onto a large ship in the port. A horse-drawn tramcar goes from the port into the city. The wheels of the horsecar don't seem to sit well on the rails; it is illuminated with a stearic candle and seems to be overcrowded. There are seven passengers in it. The men in white shirts working in the port sing something quietly to themselves. Standing by the open doors on the front platform, the conductor sings and the coachman hums along without turning away from the horses. All the horses look starved. The wheels begin to make a duller sound. We quietly roll over the bridge, catching up with and passing by the pedestrians. They too softly join in the song of the horsecar.

This is what the Rion River looks like by Poti. By Kutais it runs gurgling down, making so much noise that you can hear it even high up by the ruins that are covered, as they are supposed to be, in ivy. The ivy takes firm hold of the stone with its green claws. You can still see the angles of the vaults that have been preserved somehow. The capitals with their belt-like ornaments are lying in the grass.

We are filming the ruins. The cameraman suggests that the old monk—the only person who remains by the ruins, stage a conversation with the children. The old man sits down. His long gray sidelocks are tucked behind his ears like *payos*, and when he starts saying something to the children, I recognize the old intonation: "What are you saying?" It turns out he was saying: "Children, the church is a temple," and so on. It was the same phrase that I knew throughout my childhood from a textbook— the law of God. The old man couldn't improvise anything else.

The children were all very different: one spoke fast in Georgian, then switched to Russian for me. "Where are you from?" I asked him. "From the Saratov province. I was sent here during the evacuation." Then he looked at me, thinking how to occupy a Russian man with a conversation and asked: "Are there kindergartens in Russia?" Then he left. The orphanage is located near the ruins and from there you can see the Rion and the cornfields, and you can also hear the sounds of the song "Kirpichiki" ("Little Bricks") performed by the philharmonic orchestra.

The houses in Kutais are built on four legs, they have no solid foundation. There are also small structures similar to city houses, but in general—the houses on legs are typical Georgian rural dwellings, though they have chimneys, while the ones in Guria don't. The fences are made of wood, held together with iron wires. They are not painted and they are damp from all the rains. Irrigation ditches are covered with limestone slabs worn down by people's footsteps. In some parts the slabs have caved in and those parts are fenced off with solid, gray fences that have turned black with time.

"Do you want cigarettes?" A voice asked me from above. There was no one around. I looked up—the seller was sitting on the second floor, while his stand was on the sidewalk. I don't know how exactly he managed to sell from the second floor, as I don't smoke.

In the city there are many small smithies inside the shops. There is a market where people sell onions, cheese, and live hens, calmly lying on the ground with tied feet. People buy the hens and carry them away holding by their feet, their heads upside down. The hens keep silent, they apparently respect the local custom.

There are many black phaetons, handsomely upholstered with green and red velvet on the inside. They remind me simultaneously of galoshes and illuminations.

I lived in a small house with a long garden behind it, where the roses were almost done blooming, and small, velvety grapes were turning green.

Inside the house, there was a swing with pillows, photographs, and all this reminded me of Finland—the garden, the calm landlady, and when I entered the house, I wanted to ask in Finnish: "Ono kamori?" ("Do you have a room?").

They also forge iron in Kutais like they used to forge iron in Persia, and they shoe their buffalo in a very clumsy way by throwing the animals on their side and raising their tied feet sideways. And here in this city, or nearby, they are constructing the enormous Rion Hydroelectric Station.

Working on the construction site, graduates of higher-educational institutions turn the drilling machines by hand. They cut the rock at a thirty-degree angle with diamond core drilling crowns. The extracted rock cores are long, rough stone columns.

These people have already been drilling in the Kursk Magnetic Anomaly, somewhere in Armenia, and somewhere in the Urals. They are specialists in drilling. They will have an engine tomorrow, but they have already started drilling today.

A group of people with briefcases arrived by train—a tight, organized company. They are engineers who have finished building the ZAGES and came here with layouts and couriers ready to assemble the Rion Station.

Then members of the government arrived. There was a parade, people made speeches. Kalinin pushed a button, and three explosions started the tunnel through which the water was supposed to go somewhere outside the city.

I don't know where the electricity will go—they will probably build factories around the power station. Until then there is a small textile factory here and the Georgian Silk Factory (Gruzsholk), which buys cocoons from the peasants. They put male and female silkworms (they have wings) into a small paper bag. That's how their romance begins. There are six millions of such bags.

ADJARISTAN

The city of Batum lies along the coast of the Black Sea, which sometimes appears blue, at other times green. The mountains are moving closer to the sea. In some parts they are even piercing the sea, but in other parts they are retreating, leaving red porous valleys behind them. Everything that grows on this moist red soil is very green. There are many trees and especially palm trees. And rivers.

The rivers flow into the sea, but sometimes they don't reach it. The sea washes them out, and then they turn into swamps.

Batum is quiet now. Batumians assure that grass does grow in the city. There are boulevards with magnolias. It is a flower that resembles the lily, only it grows on a tree as big as the linden tree. The leaves on this tree are made of green leather—they are thick, and the flowers too are thick and corpulent. Bananas grow here too, but they don't have enough time to ripen. The cactus blooms once a year with a gigantic, sazhen-long flower, which looks like a dry fir tree. Batumians assert that this happens once in a hundred years.

That is not true, but for some reason people want a flower, for example, *Victoria regia*, to bloom once in a hundred years. *Victoria regia* too blooms once a year. Clearly people want to see rarities.

I went to the Women's Department of the Communist Party (Zhenotdel) in Batum with a friend. "We, the women of Adjaristan," a blond woman dictated to another woman, "protest against the intervention in China and against the presidency of … —I will correct the rest … —What do you want, Comrade?"

Together we went to the prosecutor who began telling about the new Adjarian custom—the means to fight blood feud: the co-villagers burn the house of the person in question to apparently deprive the avenger of the pleasure of honor killing. Generally incendiarism is accepted here. They burn, for example, women who have dishonored their families.

What about in the mountains? Do they sell women there? What is happening there? They don't know much about this in Batum. The prosecutor told us: "Here you only know what is said at the trial, but you won't learn anything from the cases— here they are."

They continue to abduct women, which is followed by blood feuds, but if you find and rescue a woman, she says that she consented or that she had consented earlier, and she is escorted by sixteen or more armed men.

They often tell anecdotes about Adjaristan. Lodged in the mountains and standing in opposition to the local way of life, the Soviet rule as if invokes the telling of such anecdotes.

Adjaristan didn't leave an impression of an anecdotal country on me. They are transforming it, but they are doing it through a simple and powerful means—the power station.

They have started cultivating twenty thousand and in the future a hundred thousand desyatins of tea plantations. This will cover one-fourth of the tea consumption in the Soviet Union. The country will change in any case, and these blood feuds are only dead horses running on the battlefield that don't know yet they have been killed. Something else is alive here—that which does not exist yet.

It is eighty versts from Batum to Khulo—that's in the middle of the country—along the Adjaristskhali River by car. The driver is Adjarian. An ordinary driver, an ordinary broken-down car that makes one wonder how it's still driving. I am traveling with a friend, and there is an old woman in the car who is going to see her son-in-law, a border guard. She has in her hands the most uncomfortable thing in Adjaristan in terms of car size—a large bamboo chair, which gets in everyone's way.

"It is more convenient to drive a rich person," says the driver. "Such a man has two wives in the mountains and one in Batum, or sometimes even three. He has the car to himself in Batum. Rides with his three women and sings all the time."

Adjarian women in Batum walk around in black covers. In some areas these covers are starting to degenerate, meaning they are not covering the entire face, only parts of it, and mostly for shielding from the sun.

Soon this too will become only a gesture, and instead Adjarian women will start resting their cheek on their palm. But even in the train you often meet a woman who is totally covered in a chador as though she were a chandelier protected from flies.

Men's clothing necessarily includes a bashlyk hood. Many men today wear long socks over their breeches that are held up by garters and if they are traveling by train, they tuck their train ticket under the garter. It is even elegant.

And so, after passing the yellow (from the clay soil) or maybe red pea fields the car goes uphill. We encounter rocks, trees, and ox-carts.

We reach the Kurds. The Kurds had left two months ago for the higher pastures, taking their livestock up to the alpine meadows for grazing. They pass the winters by the sea.

The old bridge across the Adjaristskhali River is simply a long log. Next to it stand new, wide bridges made of reinforced concrete, built by the Soviet government. In front of one such bridge, not too far off from the town of Keddy, there are two houses crammed with wheels. It turns out that this is the place where migrant shepherds take off the wheels from their ox-carts for storage and continue their journey on their animals across the bridge to the mountains. Many people are involved in contraband here, because the Turkish border is only seven versts away. The lights of the contrabandists flash like fireflies at night.

The fireflies start to glow at twilight and create the impression of pulling a golden thread through some fabric right in front of your eyes. It is just an insect that flies and twinkles occasionally. This type of thread was called "spun gold" in the past. Here gold is spun by the fireflies and contrabandists.

I saw very few men wearing worsted wool pants.

But the residents carry umbrellas.

The road is functional—not a bad highway.

Going higher, past Adjarian women bathing in striped chadors in mineral-rich spring waters, past houses on four legs, we enter the second town of Adjaristan. There must be some fifty houses in this town called Khulo. From here we decided not to go straight, to Abastuman, but sideways, through Gedersky Pass and the mountainous resort of Bakhmaro, down to Guria.

It is a less traveled road.

There is a stone house built by a local bey in Khulo. According to legend, every passerby had to donate a stone for the construction of this house. It is a very ordinary house the size of a rural drugstore.

Adjarians are so not used to building that the legend is taller than the house.

In Khulo there is a surgical hospital that also operates on women. They even had a midwife who was expelled, it appears, for doing abortions. The patients in the surgical hospital lie in their beds and wait bravely for their operation. People have respect for surgery and undergo operations willingly. They usually come here in terrible conditions. The patients are in hospital gowns and bashlyk hoods, which they refuse to take off. You can apparently take off the bashlyk hood of an Adjarian only when he is under anesthesia.

The local power station is halfway on the road to Guria. The Adjaristskhali River is making a knot here. They have dug out a tunnel in this place and the river will flow through the mountain. The waterfall is going to be very high. The dams will be small, and there will be three tunnels in all. The power station will be tucked away in the mountains, and it will be completely invisible once they clear the barracks. The tunnel is already finished. A rockfall during the construction killed four workers and an engineer. I heard about the catastrophe and the deaths from several people in the deadest parts of Adjaristan.

I don't know where the electric power will go. It is assumed that they will electrify the port and drain the Adjarian swamps to gain more land and root out malaria. And in Gedersky Pass people are patiently awaiting the advent of tramcars and the construction of a beech furniture factory.

From Khulo we rode on horses—also a good road—eight versts to Gorjomi village. Here lives a famous mullah—a scholar, wise man, who has seven wives and can't have more because there are seven days in the week, and succession is important to a Muslim. The mullah completed the set recently—married his seventh wife. But they say that when he unveiled his new wife's face, she looked at him and said: "You look like my father." Then the mullah let her go, because her statement might have sounded like an insinuation of incest, or maybe the mullah lacked enthusiasm that day.

He paid her a *mahr*. And a mahr is the following—as it is rather easy to divorce and forget a wife in Gorjomi and deprive her of her place in succession, the husband is required to provide for her rights and pays a fine for the divorce to her parents, which is a very high payment that can ruin a middle household.

As we had different state documents on us while traveling, they kept reassuring us that mahr didn't exist, that nobody made payments to women in Gorjomi. Who knows! But mahr seems like a good idea.

You can finally understand under Gorjomi why Adjarians need umbrellas. It is always foggy here. The Russian word *tuman* (fog), by the way, is either a Turkish or a Tatar word, everyone understands it, but they don't speak a word of Russian.

Everyone knows Georgian.

Men know Turkish. Regarding Russian words, one man—when I was parting with him—said to me timidly: "Zdravstvuyte," which is a greeting.

The houses in Gorjomi are two-storied, built with thick boards. The sloping roofs are made of stone. Flat roofs are replaced with narrow balconies without railing. The balconies are used by women, who sit there and spin wool. They are not really covering their faces with chadors, but rather protecting themselves from the sun.

The roads in the village are sloped uphill and they are so steep that you have to pull the horse by the bridle. If you are going uphill on horseback, you need to hold on to the mane. Of course, I am a bad equestrian, but I think that the vertical distance between the horse's front and back legs is about an arshin.

There is not a single flat spot in the village. Instead of a cross-road—you see bifurcations into all directions. There is very little land for cultivation and everything is fenced in. The huts are big.

We were received by the head of the Village Executive Committee.

He has a special room for guests, and I think that all in all there must have been some eight rooms in the house. They brought out horses for us from the lower level. The log granaries stand separately. The guest room is furnished with a low table made from a single piece of wood, two carpets, a kerosene lamp, a small shelf on the wall with only one glass on it from which we drank water, taking turns.

They fed us with cheese fried in butter, kefir, and cornbread—*mchadi*.

Our host had four brothers, one of whom sat with the guests while the rest stood by the table.

We took the horses in the morning and continued our way. The road followed a stream up a gorge.

The stream rolled down and meandered away from us only once in order to turn the small vertically standing mill; it simply pushed a wheel, hitting against the bent blades. The coefficient of useful action was probably five percent. Along the road we saw oxen that pulled massive red logs on a chain. When the road turned into a pathway, there were ruts on the ground from dragging those logs.

The forest here is full of red tree corpses and enormous stumps. This must have been a yew tree forest—it has been cut down and for some reason the tree trunks haven't been removed and now it's overgrowing with spruces. But the spruces below look like tall Adjarian haystacks, only their tops have been cut down. The women gathering the hay are dressed up in their best clothes, because people usually see them only during work, and it is customary to dress well at work. The road crawls up. It is foggy below, and when the fog moves, you can see what is commonly called horizon in stories, and further beyond stretch the snow-capped mountains. On the sides grow yellow lilac and other colored bushes, the leaves of which resemble the metallic garlands in the cemetery.

I am riding along with Comrade Machavariani. He knows how to ride on horseback, while I feel like a student, whose math teacher came and sat next to him—the horse knows so much more about riding than I do. She doesn't listen to me, but she rides decently. The road veers up the mountain; there are no more bushes here. We are in the meadows. It is mostly red and white clover, I don't know if they sow clover here. They do sow golden grass along the Georgian Military Highway and it blocks out the mountains rather well, but it doesn't seem that they sow clover here.

Higher up we meet a family on a sled. The runners of the sled are as wide as a palm and made of oak timber. Wife, husband, and child—they are all sitting on a round cardboard. The whole installation is pulled by a pair of oxen. A few more trees—the last ones. There are wooden boxes on the trees, tucked between the branches—these are the local beehives. They are placed really high so the bears won't reach them. They are also placed on rocks, and taken down at night when the bees are asleep.

There is a professional beekeeper and an apiary with Dadant hives and fixed-frame hives down in Khulo.

Some people own up to two hundred such hives.

We go higher. Grasslands. I had left in a crochet skullcap and canvas boots. It is cold. We are starting to see patches of snow. Initially we see snow visors over the stream, then flat and glossy arches like those in Persian baths. The stream runs underneath the ice. We go even higher. We meet Adjarians on horseback;

one is wearing a handkerchief knotted on four corners on his head instead of a bashlyk hood. Two of them are wearing overcoats, and one is wearing a mackintosh. They are wearing twill pants—made of local wool, coarse material, very narrow. They all have large satchels made of whole calfskins. They are transporting butter in them to Bakhmaro.

The horse is finally walking on snow. We are very tired, but we keep going. We start to descend, and here in the valley that looks like two closed hands is the second Gorjomi. It is the same village but in summertime. The cattle are grazing. There are two-storied houses without windows. The long slots instead of windows are about one and a half fingers wide. The thick logs that replace the stairs are placed at forty-five-degree angles, and they have notches cut out on them. It is rather easy to walk here. Children are running. The air is remarkably clean and transparent. People come here for the summer.

We continue to descend—gnarled birches, spruces start to appear, and we finally come down to the resort of Bakhmaro, which is at two versts above sea level. It is surrounded with spruces, the houses are newly built.

Approximately twelve thousand people come through here during the summer season. The sun is so strong here that my companion, who didn't get sunburned anywhere on the road, got sunburned in the fog in two hours.

Here the sun is like a quartz lamp.

A Gurian man is sitting by the road and singing, while grilling a piglet. When he is done blowing on the coals, he takes out a pipe, leans it against his cheek, and begins to sing some couplets, while moving his fingers over the holes on the pipe. That's how he sings, accompanying himself on the wind instrument.

The descent from Bakhmaro is through a beech tree forest. The forest sits on the hill like a horse-rider in a saddle when

going down—i.e. the trees grow slanted in order to stand vertically on the hillside. The forest stretches for twelve versts. The
trunks are gray and the foliage is still covered in thick beard-like
moss. The horse climbs down, stepping between the roots of the
trees. You can get down in five hours if you rush the horse. In
some parts the road is cut across by narrow trenches in which
a rider can be completely invisible. Sometimes the trenches are
two sazhens deep. They are muddy due to the rains.

You keep going down. It gets dark, and the spun gold of the
fireflies begins to glow in front of your eyes, while you meet people going up to the resort. Old women riding on top of packs,
children tied tightly to the horses with ropes. This is apparently
a repetition of the nomadic migration. People go up to the resort
like the Kurds migrating to their summer pastures. It is more like
a resettlement than a trip to a resort.

We go down. We have already passed sixty-five versts in a day.
We are so tired that we can't even get off our horses and we drink
tea by the taverns while sitting in our saddles, because we don't
know how to get off. We continue our descent. It is completely
dark, but my horse, which as you know is a math professor, low-
ers her head and sniffs the road. Suddenly, a completely strange
sensation. The ground is level. We have reached Guria.

A leading figure in the Russian Formalist movement of the 1920s, Viktor Shklovsky (1893-1984) had a profound effect on twentieth-century Russian literature. Several of his books have been translated into English, including *Theory of Prose*, *Knight's Move*, and *A Hunt for Optimism*, all available from Dalkey Archive Press.

Shushan Avagyan translates from Armenian and Russian. She is the translator of Viktor Shklovsky's *Bowstring: On the Dissimilarity of the Similar*, *A Hunt for Optimism*, and other works available from Dalkey Archive Press.